A PERFECT WAY TO HEAVEN

BARBARA CARTLAND

Barbaracartland.com Ltd

First published on the internet in March 2008
by Barbaracartland.com

ISBN 978-1-905155-92-7

The characters and situations in this book are entirely imaginary and bear no relation to any real person or actual happening.

Printed and bound in Great Britain by Cle-Print Ltd,
St Ives, Cambridgeshire.

A PERFECT WAY TO HEAVEN

Prince Charles de Courel was lavishly dressed from top to toe in a red jacket and epaulettes. A black cape was thrown aside over one shoulder and he had removed his white gloves and tucked them under his arm.

Diamond rings winked on his fingers and even the buttons of his cuffs seemed to flash showing that they too were of precious stones.

His hair was gold and his eyes were grey.

'Grey as goose-down,' thought Elvira dreamily.

He was her every idea of a real Prince and for the first time in her life she longed to possess what was not in her power to possess. How she would love to be courted by just such a lofty personage.

'*If he would only look my way once*,' she prayed fervently, quite forgetting her sombre dress and appearance.

THE BARBARA CARTLAND PINK COLLECTION

Titles in this series

1. The Cross of Love
2. Love in the Highlands
3. Love Finds the Way
4. The Castle of Love
5. Love is Triumphant
6. Stars in the Sky
7. The Ship of Love
8. A Dangerous Disguise
9. Love Became Theirs
10. Love Drives In
11. Sailing to Love
12. The Star of Love
13. Music is the Soul of Love
14. Love in the East
15. Theirs to Eternity
16. A Paradise on Earth
17. Love Wins in Berlin
18. In Search of Love
19. Love Rescues Rosanna
20. A Heart in Heaven
21. The House of Happiness
22. Royalty Defeated by Love
23. The White Witch
24. They Sought Love
25. Love is the Reason for Living
26. They Found Their Way to Heaven
27. Learning to Love
28. Journey to Happiness
29. A Kiss in the Desert
30. The Heart of Love
31. The Richness of Love
32. For Ever and Ever
33. An Unexpected Love
34. Saved by an Angel
35. Touching the Stars
36. Seeking Love
37. Journey to Love
38. The Importance of Love
39. Love by the Lake
40. A Dream Come True
41. The King without a Heart
42. The Waters of Love
43. Danger to the Duke
44. A Perfect way to Heaven

THE BARBARA CARTLAND PINK COLLECTION

Barbara Cartland was the most prolific bestselling author in the history of the world. She was frequently in the Guinness Book of Records for writing more books in a year than any other living author. In fact her most amazing literary feat was when her publishers asked for more Barbara Cartland romances, she doubled her output from 10 books a year to over 20 books a year, when she was 77.

She went on writing continuously at this rate for 20 years and wrote her last book at the age of 97, thus completing 400 books between the ages of 77 and 97.

Her publishers finally could not keep up with this phenomenal output, so at her death she left 160 unpublished manuscripts, something again that no other author has ever achieved.

Now the exciting news is that these 160 original unpublished Barbara Cartland books are already being published and by Barbaracartland.com exclusively on the internet, as the international web is the best possible way of reaching so many Barbara Cartland readers around the world.

The 160 books are published monthly and will be numbered in sequence.

The series is called the Pink Collection as a tribute to Barbara Cartland whose favourite colour was pink and it became very much her trademark over the years.

The Barbara Cartland Pink Collection is published only on the internet. Log on to www.barbaracartland.com to find out how you can purchase the books monthly as they are published, and take out a subscription that will ensure that all subsequent editions are delivered to you by mail order to your home.

NEW

Barbaracartland.com is proud to announce the publication of ten new Audio Books for the first time as CDs. They are favourite Barbara Cartland stories read by well-known actors and actresses and each story extends to 4 or 5 CDs. The Audio Books are as follows :

The Patient Bridegroom
A Challenge of Hearts
A Train to Love
The Unbroken Dream
The Cruel Count
The Passion and the Flower
Little White Doves of Love
The Prince and the Pekinese
A King in Love
A Sign of Love

More Audio Books will be published in the future and the above titles can be purchased by logging on to the website www.barbaracartland.com or please write to the address below.

If you do not have access to a computer, you can write for information about the Barbara Cartland Pink Collection and the Barbara Cartland Audio Books to the following address :

Barbara Cartland.com Ltd.
Camfield Place,
Hatfield,
Hertfordshire AL9 6JE
United Kingdom.
Telephone:+44 (0)1707 642629
Fax:+44 (0)1707 663041

THE LATE DAME BARBARA CARTLAND

Barbara Cartland who sadly died in May 2000 at the age of nearly 99 was the world's most famous romantic novelist who wrote 723 books in her lifetime with worldwide sales of over 1 billion copies and her books were translated into 36 different languages.

As well as romantic novels, she wrote historical biographies, 6 autobiographies, theatrical plays, books of advice on life, love, vitamins and cookery. She also found time to be a political speaker and television and radio personality.

She wrote her first book at the age of 21 and this was called *Jigsaw*. It became an immediate bestseller and sold 100,000 copies in hardback and was translated into 6 different languages. She wrote continuously throughout her life, writing bestsellers for an astonishing 76 years. Her books have always been immensely popular in the United States, where in 1976 her current books were at numbers 1 & 2 in the B. Dalton bestsellers list, a feat never achieved before or since by any author.

Barbara Cartland became a legend in her own lifetime and will be best remembered for her wonderful romantic novels, so loved by her millions of readers throughout the world.

Her books will always be treasured for their moral message, her pure and innocent heroines, her good looking and dashing heroes and above all her belief that the power of love is more important than anything else in everyone's life.

"Life without love is no life at all."

Barbara Cartland

CHAPTER ONE
1849

Elvira Carrisford repressed a yawn.

She had been travelling since early morning and the air in the coach was stale. The plump lady opposite had insisted that the windows be kept closed all the way for fear of catching a chill in the November air.

Besides the plump lady there was a cleric, who licked his finger every time he turned a page in his missal, a farmer's wife who shared out her loaf of bread and cheese when everyone started to get hungry, two spinster sisters with yellow mittens and a young man and a young lady in whom Elvira felt a particular interest.

These two looked at each other so often and with such devotion that she was certain they were eloping.

The young man's shirt cuffs were ragged and his boots were scuffed. He was obviously poor and the young lady looked as if she came from a more significant background.

She wore calf leather shoes and her hands were thrust deep into a white fur muff. Elvira decided that the young lady's parents had objected to her interest in the lowly clerk and so she had agreed to run away with him.

Elvira watched intently as the young man gently rearranged the young lady's cloak about her shoulders.

With a pang she wondered if anyone would ever look at her in such an adoring manner.

She turned her head and stared out of the grimy window. The reason she found the young couple so fascinating was that they made her think of her own parents. They too had eloped. Her father had been poor – a musician, not a clerk and her mother had come from a well-to-do and disapproving family.

Elvira wondered if her mother had worn calf leather shoes on *her* flight and if her father's boots had been scuffed and his cuffs ragged.

She sighed and leaned her head against the window.

She had never known her father. He had died before she was born. Her mother had died two years later and Elvira had been brought up by her mother's elder sister, Aunt Willis.

Aunt Willis had never married. She disliked men almost as much as she disliked children and she had not been particularly pleased to be entrusted with little Elvira, but she was a religious woman and considered it her duty. It was also her duty to ensure that Elvira was brought up in such a way that she would never make the same mistake as her mother, Winona.

"*If* one had to marry," said Aunt Willis – and she supposed that most girls, being of a weak disposition, could think of nothing else in life – "*if* one had to marry, then let it to be a gentleman such as my elder sister Wilhelmina had married."

She had married Lord Baseheart, a rich and powerful grandee with a handsome castle and vast lands in the County of Herefordshire and not an impecunious, sickly musician like Elvira's father, who could not even live long enough to see his daughter brought into the world!

"My poor, silly sister Winona!" Aunt Willis would often lament to Elvira. "I am sure she would be alive now if it was not for you and your father. His death broke her spirit and your birth weakened her body. Nobody could save her!"

Here Aunt Willis would pause and blow her long bony nose.

"But – but at least they both knew what it was to love," Elvira once unwisely ventured.

"Love!" exploded Aunt Willis. "Pah! An over-rated emotion. Be sure you never succumb."

Elvira thought it unlikely she ever would succumb, since it was Aunt Willis's habit never to invite anyone under sixty to visit.

Moreover, Aunt Willis so disapproved of love and romance that she went out of her way to ensure that Elvira never thought of herself as a candidate for such nonsense. She kept only one mirror in the house and that was so cracked and mottled with age that it was almost impossible to determine one's own features in its depths.

Since no young person came to the house there was never anyone to quarrel with Aunt Willis's assessment of Elvira's beauty, or lack of it, or proffer the temptation of a pocket mirror.

The only time Elvira ever met anyone her own age was the one occasion when Aunt Willis decided to make the long journey west to Baseheart Castle to visit her remaining sister, Wilhelmina. Elvira went too and met her cousin Delphine, the daughter of Aunt Wilhelmina and Lord Baseheart.

Baseheart!

With a finger, Elvira idly traced the name on the steamy carriage window.

She remembered spires and turrets and long corridors silent as the tomb along which she and Delphine had chased each other like puppies. She remembered silk sheets and hot chocolate and her Aunt Wilhelmina coming to tuck her in at night. She had kissed the tip of her nose and whispered that she was going to grow up a beauty like her mother.

"Oh, I don't think so," responded the four year old Elvira with great solemnity. "My nose is too snub and my hair too red. Aunt Willis said so."

A frown had crossed Aunt Wilhelmina's features.

"Perhaps you need to spend more time here at Baseheart with us. You will soon have a better opinion of yourself. I will make sure that Lord Baseheart invites you next summer."

Alas that invitation never came. Aunt Wilhelmina became ill and had to spend most of her time abroad. Delphine remained at Baseheart with her indulgent father.

Then news came that Aunt Wilhelmina had died. Aunt Willis attended the funeral, but after that there was little correspondence between herself and her wealthy brother-in-law.

Elvira rather suspected that Lord Baseheart found Aunt Willis too disapproving. She remembered Aunt Willis coughing loudly whenever Lord Baseheart took out a cigar, and tut-tutting even more loudly when he reached for the sherry.

At all events, Elvira had never been back to Baseheart Castle again. Until now!

Five days ago a letter had arrived for Aunt Willis from Lord Baseheart. She had turned it over and over in her hand in astonishment.

"Wonders will never cease!" she sighed.

At last she opened it, adjusted her lorgnette and read aloud over the teacups.

"*My dear sister-in-law,*

My daughter Delphine is now of an age to marry. I have sought high and low for someone I consider worthy of her hand and at last I have found him. His name is Charles Rowland, a distant Baseheart relation. He also happens to be, through his mother's side of the family, nephew and sole heir to Prince Louis de Courel.

The inheritance depends entirely on Charles marrying whomsoever the Prince decrees and out of fond friendship with myself, he decrees that his nephew should marry my daughter. I have no doubt that when the young man in question sets eyes on my daughter, a great beauty, madam, and of uncommon intelligence, as I am sure you will recall – he will feel the alliance to be more of a pleasure than a duty."

Here Aunt Willis lowered her lorgnette with a grunt.

"From what I have heard of that young creature, Delphine, he will be more likely to want to run a mile. Lord Baseheart has indulged her every whim since her mother died. She has only to click her fingers and she has her heart's desire. On top of that, her eyes are too close together."

"Are they, aunt? I don't remember," said Elvira politely.

"Well, take it from me, they are!" sniffed Aunt Willis. "Believe you me, the draw here is not the charms of Delphine Baseheart, but rather the chink of her father's money. The French aristocracy lost more than some of their heads in the Revolution, you know."

"But the Revolution was over half a century ago, aunt," commented Elvira as she reached for the sugar bowl.

"That may be!" retorted Aunt Willis. "But they never managed to recover *all* their wealth. Still it *would* be something of a coup to have a Prince in the family."

"What else does the letter say, aunt?"

Aunt Willis raised her lorgnette again and read on,

"*Charles Rowland is coming to Baseheart next week to meet his intended. My widowed sister, Lady Cruddock, is now in constant residence at Baseheart and has hitherto proved an admirable chaperone for Delphine.*

Nevertheless, my daughter has now taken it into her head that she wants a companion of her own age when the Prince is here. It is with this in mind that I have taken up my pen to write to you.

Elvira is only a year younger than my daughter and would, I believe, be a suitable companion. Should the post suit Elvira, I would ask her to join us at Baseheart before the week is out. I believe the opportunity is too great for her to refuse.

Yours etc.

Rupert Baseheart. "

Elvira's eyes widened as her aunt read out this last part of the letter.

"But I *do* refuse! I don't want to leave here and I don't want to leave *you.*"

Aunt Willis regarded her sternly.

"Elvira, you are now eighteen years of age. God

knows that I have done my duty, but I want a life unencumbered with the worries of rearing a young girl of no means and little personal attractions. It may be that at Baseheart Castle you will encounter some young man, a secretary in his Lordship's employ perhaps – who will see more in you than meets the eye. You cannot expect a Prince, after all!"

Elvira had listened bleakly.

"Don't you – care for me at all, aunt?"

Aunt Willis set her lips firmly.

"I daresay I shall find the house rather quiet after you go, but I'll get used to it."

"G-go?" repeated Elvira. "I am truly to go, then?"

"Yes," insisted Aunt Willis impatiently. "Haven't I indicated that? We must sort through your wardrobe this morning. This afternoon I shall write a reply to Lord Baseheart and tell him to expect you on Wednesday."

In fact it had taken a day or two longer than expected to organise the journey.

Elvira was to take the coach to Gloucester, but was to stop at the *White Doe Inn* on the road to the Forest of Dean. There the Baseheart carriage would meet her and convey her on the last three hour lap to the castle.

Aunt Willis had purchased a second-hand trunk and a couple of carpet bags for Elvira's belongings, which did not amount to much. Along with the usual camisoles and cotton under-bodices there were three dresses. These were all blue, which Aunt Willis deemed a perfectly reliable colour.

Besides, she added somewhat grudgingly, they matched Elvira's sapphire eyes, her only redeeming feature!

It had been a shock to Elvira to find that Aunt Willis had been only too happy to part with her. She had never been demonstrative and often made sharp remarks, but nevertheless she and Elvira had managed to muddle along with little actual friction.

It had been a lonely life for Elvira, but she was aware that many young girls were far less lucky. At least Aunt Willis had provided her with a governess – the elderly, short-sighted but kindly Miss Hoot, who had taught Elvira reading, writing and arithmetic.

There were no books at Aunt Willis's except the Bible and theological tracts, but Miss Hoot had dared to smuggle in some fairy tales and one or two classics such as *Gulliver's Travels.* She had not, however, taught Elvira any languages, not even Latin or Greek, which Elvira regretted.

Remembering the letter from Delphine she had received the day before, her face clouded. She had not formed a favourable impression of her cousin's character from the letter's style and content.

Elvira sighed again. She was beginning to rub out the word *Baseheart* that she had traced on the steamy window when a voice hailed out from the coachman's box.

"*White Doe Inn* approaching!"

Disregarding the health of the plump lady in her sudden excitement, Elvira threw down the window and peered out.

A moment later and she gave a start. It was late afternoon and the pale sun was sinking, but even so she could detect the black cloud of smoke that hovered over the roof of the galleried building ahead.

*

The *White Doe Inn* appeared to be on fire –

The yard of the inn was in chaos. Figures with soot-smeared faces ran to and fro with pails, water slopping over the sides onto the cobbles. The air smelt of burnt wood.

A stable boy ran up to the coach and lowered the step for Elvira to descend as the other passengers peered after her through the open door.

"What happened here?" the coachman called out to the stable boy.

The boy, with soot-ringed eyes, grinned.

"Fire in the kitchen, sir. It was all 'ands to help, us workers and the guests alike. It's more nor less out. We're just damping it down."

Elvira looked about her in dismay. There was no sign of the Baseheart carriage.

"Only you, miss?" asked the stable boy.

The coachman answered for her. "She's all."

The boy gestured to another young fellow like himself and the two of them hauled down Elvira's trunk and bags. The first boy then slammed the carriage door before Elvira could bid farewell to her fellow passengers.

The coachman cracked his whip and the coach wheeled round. It quickly passed out under the archway, carrying away plump lady, cleric, spinster sisters, farmer's wife and the devoted eloping couple.

Elvira stared after it, feeling strangely desolate.

"Will you come on into the parlour?" the stable boy asked.

Elvira glanced towards the inn and shook her head.

The interior was bound to smell even more strongly of smoke than the yard. Timidly, she pressed a coin into the stable boy's palm.

"I shall sit out here on my trunk," she said. "I am expecting to be collected at any moment."

"Suit yourself, miss," he shrugged, pocketing the coin and loping off.

Elvira settled down onto her trunk, crossing her shawl more tightly on her breast. The sky was dark with something more than dusk. The air was chill and one or two tiny white flakes fluttered down through it, like the feathers of a ghostly bird. Servants began to light torches around the yard and one or two went over to the pump to wash their sooty faces.

"Fire out?" a serving wench asked them, pausing with a bag of flour balanced on her hip.

"Quite out," responded one of the two men at the pump. "Not enough flame to fry an egg now!"

The wench laughed as Elvira's eyes strayed beyond her and alighted on a tall stranger leaning against a post and wiping his brow with his sleeve.

He had obviously been helping to put out the fire, for his shirt was open at the neck and his sleeves were rolled up. His forearms looked very strong and brown and Elvira supposed he was an employee at the inn.

The wench noticed him too, as she shifted her bag of floor on her hip and sauntered over to speak to him.

Elvira wondered at her forwardness.

For some reason this scene made her think of Delphine and she turned to the reticule on her lap, opened it and took out letter she had received from her cousin.

"*Dearest Elvira,*

Papa has told me you have agreed to come and live here as my companion. What fun!

My aunt Lady Cruddock's nose is a little put out of joint, but I won't mind her and nor should you. I didn't want her watching my every move when the Prince came courting.

I do hope you're passably pretty for I don't like to look at ugly things. Why, there were mornings when the sight of my Aunt Cruddock quite turns my stomach. People say I am the perfect image of my mother and she was a great beauty.

Your mother had lovely hair, but Aunt Willis is a horror. I remember wanting to take the garden shears to those hairs on her chin!

Anyway, won't it be a lark to have a Prince here? Well, someone who is nearly a Prince. I shan't let myself love him, my aunt says that would be a huge mistake. But I shall let him love ME. Which he will do. I always have a full card at the ball. Shall I let you in on a secret? I am going to make him my slave. There! Don't be shocked. It's what all girls should do to their suitors.

Well, come quickly. I am very impatient, you know, and don't like to be kept waiting.

It's my only shortcoming, Papa says so.

Your affectionate cousin,

Delphine."

From the tone of the letter, Elvira rather doubted that impatience was Delphine's only flaw.

She stared down at the large untidy handwriting. Could she and the writer have anything in common?

She heard a rattle of wheels approach the inn and looked up expectantly. Sure enough, it was a private carriage, but as it rolled in under the arch she was certain it was not for her.

It was a rickety old-fashioned carriage, bouncing violently up and down on its springs. Its exterior was shabby and unpainted and there was no crest on its door. The two horses pulling it held the air of creatures coaxed out of retirement.

She was returning Delphine's letter to her reticule when she heard herself addressed in rather rough tones.

"You 'appen to be this Miss Elvira?"

She looked up. The driver of the rickety carriage was staring down at her.

"I – I am," she stammered with trepidation.

"I'm 'ere to take you to the castle."

"B-Baseheart?" questioned Elvira, peering at the carriage to see whether she had indeed missed a crest.

The driver seemed to know what she was seeking and gave a sly chortle.

"Oh, you won't find a crest, miss. This is the old governess's carriage that's been a-mouldering in the barn."

"I see."

"Lord Baseheart, Lady Cruddock, Miss Delphine – they were all out visitin' in theirs and the axle is off the guest carriage. And the other one's bein' polished up for the use of Mr. Charles Rowland when he comes. And the last one is too grand altogether for the present purpose. So this is what you get!"

Hiding her humiliation at not being considered important enough to be collected in a crested carriage, Elvira rose from her trunk.

"This is all I have," she gestured.

"Haul it aboard, then."

Elvira blinked. Was he not even going to help? Since the driver turned idly whistling from her she saw that no, he was not. So she dragged one of the two carpet bags over to the back of the carriage and attempted to hoist it on to the luggage rack herself.

"May I help?"

In the dimming light, Elvira made out the sooty features of the stranger who had been leaning against the post. The wench had obviously received short shrift.

"Why, thank you, yes," she said. "I should be very grateful."

The driver had stopped whistling and turned at the sound of the stranger's voice. The stranger regarded him sternly.

"Could you not have shifted yourself, man, to help the young lady?"

The driver excused himself in wheedling tones.

"I've a gammy arm. Injured at Waterloo."

The stranger raised an eyebrow.

"Indeed? You must have been very young."

"I were a lad of fourteen. The drummer boy. Played with me right 'and. Can't play no more."

He raised an arm that was indeed puckered and twisted.

The stranger's tone softened.

"No. I can see. That's hard luck on a man."

The driver was mollified.

"I'll light the lantern to 'elp you back there," he offered.

Turning, he reached for the lantern that swung at the

front of the coach and began to fumble with the wick.

The stranger meanwhile set about dealing with Elvira's luggage.

Elvira could not help but marvel at the apparent ease with which he then hoisted it up on to the rack. He paused for a moment, passing his forearm across his brow.

"I hope you haven't far to go," he said. "There's snow on the way."

"I don't know how far in miles," answered Elvira. "But I was told it would take about three hours."

The stranger gave a troubled frown.

"Three hours!" He stepped back and called up to the driver. "You surely don't intend to travel for three hours with the weather so threatening?"

"I've my orders," replied the driver loudly. "'Sides, those 'orses may look like nags but they're 'ardy."

"I shouldn't like to pass the night here anyway," put in Elvira. "Not with the fire barely out."

With a shrug, the stranger lifted the two carpet bags on top of the trunk and then he felt for the ropes that would secure the load.

"Light a-comin'," called the coachman.

Elvira looked up into the soft yellow beam. The stranger glanced her way and then looked again, as if transfixed.

She could not read his expression, since he stood outside the small circle of light, but she felt herself scrutinised. She was not accustomed to this and began to blush. Had her hair come loose under her bonnet?

The driver was growing restive.

"We've got to be off. You said yourself the weather

might turn rough. Best to get ahead of it."

The stranger stirred in the darkness.

"My humble apologies," he replied in so low a voice that the reply seemed hardly aimed at the driver's ears. "I was momentarily dazzled."

"Oh, by the light," said Elvira with an understanding nod.

"No, young lady. By you."

Elvira was astonished.

"By *me*? Why, what could dazzle you, sir, about me?"

The stranger gave a sceptical laugh .

"Come, come, young lady, you cannot be unaware of the effect of your beauty!"

"My *beauty*? You are not to mock me, sir. I know full well that I have a turned-up nose and too low a hairline."

"Too low a hairline?" echoed the stranger.

"Yes. Aunt Willis said so."

The stranger became immediately solemn.

"Oh. Aunt Willis. No arguing with her, I suspect."

"No," replied Elvira, a certain wistfulness in her voice. The stranger noticed and seemed about to respond when the driver threw out another impatient reprimand,

"What's keepin' you there?"

The stranger returned to his task without another word. He tightened the ropes around the trunk, hooking them through the handles of the carpet bags and tying them both in a firm knot.

When he had finished he wiped a hand on his shirt before extending it towards Elvira.

"Young lady."

That he had extended his hand for Elvira to shake did not occur to her. Reddening, she groped in her reticule and withdrew a coin, which she attempted to press into the stranger's palm.

He stepped back with a laugh and a shake of his head.

"It was a labour most willingly undertaken, ma'am. How could I have refused to aid a young lady possessing such – singular charms? Whatever Aunt Willis says."

He opened the carriage door and handed Elvira in. Then he closed the door behind her and strode away towards the pump.

Pressing her face to the glass, Elvira saw that the wench had reappeared and seemed to be awaiting him with a fresh towel over her arm.

He certainly seemed a cut above the usual hostelry servant, she thought. She watched as he pressed down the handle and leaned his head into the flow of water.

The carriage gave a lurch and the two horses started off with greater vigour than Elvira would have supposed possible.

The stranger looked up from the pump, his face and hair dripping, the front of his shirt drenched. It was Elvira's last image of him.

In an instant he and the wench and the still smoking inn were lost to sight.

With a heart grown suddenly heavy, Elvira turned her face towards Baseheart.

It struck her as fitting that the road ahead was dark and the moon was swallowed whole in a black and lowering sky.

CHAPTER TWO

Despite its unpromising exterior, the interior of the carriage was more comfortable than Elvira had expected. The upholstery might be worn but the seat was soft.

An image of the stranger at the pump floated before her and then she was fast asleep.

When she awoke the carriage was motionless.

She started up anxiously. Had they really reached Baseheart already? Had she slept for the whole three hours? Taking up her cape she threw it over her shoulders and turned to the window.

It was covered with ice. They must have been travelling at a slow pace indeed for the glass to ice up so much.

Reaching forward, she threw open the door.

The world outside was white. White and deathly silent. The forest ranged on all sides, trees looming petrified through the glittering flakes.

Elvira turned her head at the sound of a curse and leaned further out to see the driver leaning on the handle of a shovel, his brow shining and damp.

"What has happened?" she asked.

The driver gave a surly grunt.

"The carriage 'it a drift. I 'ad a shovel on the box, but I can't dig the wheel out."

Elvira glanced fearfully about her.

"W-what shall we do?"

"We passed a cottage with a light in the window about a mile ago. I'll walk back and summon 'elp. We can't stay in the forest all night."

"I'll come with you!"

Elvira began hurriedly to put on her boots.

"That you won't," he snorted. "Your long skirts'd 'amper us. I'll go alone and you shelter 'ere in the carriage." He reached up on to the box and pulled something down. " 'Ere's a spare horse blanket. Wrap up in that."

Elvira caught the blanket. The driver leaned his shovel against the carriage, patted the horses and took down the glowing lantern from its hook.

"I'll make tracks," he said and set off.

Elvira stared after him and soon his figure was lost to sight. The glow of the lantern bobbed on for another yard or two in the swirling snow. Then it too was gone.

She was alone, more alone than she had ever been in her life. She thought of Aunt Willis in her hard-backed chair in front of the parlour fire and felt a pang of homesickness.

Aunt Willis's house had been the only home she had ever known and despite its austerity and lack of affection, Elvira felt attached to it.

She tried to think of reaching the safety of Baseheart Castle, but in her imagination its turrets and spires were no more than icy stalactites, its windows frosted and empty.

She shivered and tried to sink deeper into the

blanket. It smelled of hay and horse and its texture was rough on her chin.

The stranger had warned the driver and herself about the impending snowstorm, but they had not listened and now they were paying the price.

For a fleeting moment she imagined the stranger's arms around her, his warm body sheltering her. He had said she was beautiful, after all!

Then she felt herself blush at these unaccustomed thoughts. What would Aunt Willis say? A total stranger – a servant – a man who no doubt took the attentions of women for granted.

'It's only because I am alone and afraid that my mind is running on like this,' she thought. 'It's only because I have met hardly any young men that I am thinking of him.'

She closed her eyes and tried to sleep, but sleep would not come. She was so aware of the relentless snow outside.

After a moment she started up again with a sudden new terror. Supposing she and the carriage should be completely buried before the driver returned with help?

A howl out in the forest made her blood freeze. The carriage shifted on its axles as the horses strained anxiously in their shafts. She threw open the door and stared out. Flakes flew in, stinging her cheeks and there was now a strong wind behind the snow.

She closed the door again and threw her arms vigorously round her shoulders trying to warm herself, but it was no use. Soon she was shivering uncontrollably. Surely it would be better to be moving than sitting here?

This time when she opened the carriage door she

stepped out. She tried to walk towards the horses to see how they were faring, but the wind forced her back.

The blanket flapped about her as she turned and peered along the route the driver had taken. With the wind behind her she would surely make good time if she followed him? If he was already on his way with aid, she would meet him en route and if not better she keep moving than freeze to death inside the carriage!

She set off feeling sorry to leave the horses behind, but there was no way she could unharness them.

There was no road beneath her feet and she seemed to be walking on a thick carpet which her boots sank into at every step.

She only knew that she was indeed following the road by the trees that lined each side of the route. Their ghostly branches seemed to point the way.

She struggled on, trying to convince herself that she was making good time. Soon the lower part of her skirt became caked in snow and growing heavier by the minute.

Then the wind changed direction. It now seemed to run through the trees with a flurry and strike her front on. She turned her face away from its icy bite.

She gave a cry as the blanket was ripped from her shoulders. The snow was so blinding that she could not, dared not stop to search for it.

Her fingers clutched at her cape and the bonnet she had left behind she was certain would not have remained long on her head. Pins were snatched spitefully from her head and soon her hair was lashing at her cheeks. She reached her hands out in front of her as if to fend off blows.

Snow filled her mouth, her nostrils. Her breath

froze her lungs. Her skirts seemed to be dragging at her frame, urging her to give up, to sink down. Would it be so bad to relinquish the struggle for a little while, she asked herself. She could not turn back now.

Yet she could not go on. Her limbs were aching so and her heart seemed to labour in her breast. Why not rest? Why not sleep for a few minutes? Why not let the soft snow mantle her?

She stood swaying, buffeted, trying to think and to reason. Then slowly she sank down, down, her skirts billowing out around her. It was calmer here, the wind raged above her.

She stretched out gratefully, laying her head on a pillow of such sweet softness that she was soon drifting into sleep.

*

How long she lay there she did not know.

Dimly she heard voices in the distance but she did not rise. She thought she glimpsed a light, hovering like a great yellow moth above her.

Someone cried out "over here." And someone echoed strangely, "*par ici*, *Maître*."

'*Ici Maître*,' Elvira thought dreamily.

Someone stooped to rub her hands between his own. She knew it was a he because his hands were large and strong. This same person brushed the snow from her face and she sensed him draw off his cloak and the next moment felt it thrown over her.

An arm about her shoulders pulled her up to a sitting position and a leather bottle was held to her lips.

She drank. It was not a taste she knew, but it quickly fired her veins.

The effort of holding up her head was too much, however, and she fell back, swimming into semi-consciousness. Arms reached under her and she was lifted onto the back of a horse.

She might have fallen but that someone quickly leapt up behind her and with one hand gripped her tight about the waist.

With a barely perceptible sigh, she leaned her head against a manly breast and slept –

*

Stirring awake, Elvira's first thought was that she was warm. Warm! It was a glorious feeling.

She opened her eyes and saw a fire leaping merrily in a large stone hearth.

Her eyes travelled upwards to where a skirt hung on a drying rack. She blinked and looked more closely. It was her own skirt!

She looked down. She was in an armchair and a cushion had been set behind her head and a plaid shawl over her knees. Another shawl was around her shoulders and beneath these she wore only her petticoat and stiff under-bodice.

An eerily familiar voice spoke from the silence.

"*You are awake*?"

She turned with a start and there, opposite her, on a wooden pew with legs thrust out before him, lounged the stranger from the *White Doe Inn*.

His left hand dangled an empty wine glass and his glittering dark eyes were trained intently on her face. She had the impression he had been watching her as she slept.

Her heart quailed. Surely she was not alone here with this man – stripped as she was to her undergarments!

Was it he who had removed her skirt and blouse?

Face flushing, she clutched the shawl tighter to her trembling breast.

The stranger seemed to divine her fears.

"Do not agitate yourself," he said softly. "You have a chaperone."

Elvira looked wildly round and sure enough, in a shadowy corner of the room sat an old woman in a mob cap. Her gnarled hands lay in her lap and her chin rested on her chest.

"She is asleep," Elvira observed uneasily.

"Ah, that I cannot help," smiled the stranger. "Shall I clap my hands and startle her awake?"

Elvira looked again at the old woman.

"That would be cruel," she replied.

"My thought entirely." The stranger held up his glass. "Would you care for some liquid refreshment?"

Elvira shook her head.

"What I should like – is to know where I am."

"Why," answered the stranger, gesturing towards the sleeping woman, "in that kind lady's cottage."

Elvira looked around the room. It was indeed no more than a cottage with walls of whitewashed stone and cured hams hung from the low rafters. A ladder in a corner led up to a loft and no doubt that was where the only bed was located.

It was unmistakably a peasant's dwelling and the old woman was a peasant woman. It seemed most gallant of the stranger to call her a lady.

"Did she – undress me?" she asked tentatively.

The stranger took a sip of wine. He seemed amused

by her discomfiture.

“She did indeed. I promise you we withdrew to the garden, despite the blizzard.”

Elvira considered this. ‘We?’ A phrase floated into her memory. ‘*Ici Maître*.’

“You mean you and your – Master?”

“Me and my – ?” For a moment the stranger looked puzzled. Then his face cleared and a twinkle appeared in his eye. “Yes. Just so. Me and my Master.”

“Was it he who brought me here? On his horse?”

“It was indeed – the Master – who brought you here.”

“I should like to thank him. W-where is he now?”

“My – Master – has gone with a note to fetch the doctor.”

Elvira wondered that the Master did not see fit to send his servant rather than go himself, but still she was glad it had been a somewhat familiar face she had seen when she first awoke.

“How is it that – you and – he came across me in the snow? The last I saw of you was at the *White Doe Inn*. It did not seem then that you intended to travel on. Indeed you thought my driver foolish to ignore the signs of bad weather ahead.”

“My – Master and I had merely stopped at the inn for supper when the fire broke out and we helped fight it. Once it was out my – Master decided to continue with his plan to reach Gloucester and spend the night there.

“We took a wrong turn and found ourselves on the forest road and we reined in at this cottage to ask directions. Then your driver appeared seeking help and the old lady directed him to a nearby cottage where three strong young labourers live.

"I am sure he and they are even now hauling the carriage from the snow. My – Master and I, meanwhile, rode straight out to rescue you."

Elvira murmured her gratitude. Her moment of lucidity was over and during the stranger's explanation both he and the room had begun to swim.

Her breath had quickened and she felt feverish and when a knock came at the door it sounded like a bone on a muffled drum.

She was aware of the stranger rising and dimly aware of two figures entering amid a flurry of snow.

'The stranger's Master,' she thought, 'returning with the doctor.'

She had not the strength to focus on the figure of this elusive Master or note his features. She could barely keep her eyes open and her head seemed to grow heavy.

The old woman must have awakened, for now she came limping into view to relieve the doctor of his cape. At a nod from him the stranger and his Master departed, disappearing into the fierce white storm outside.

The doctor approached Elvira and his face with its stern brow and grizzled beard loomed over her.

"And how are you feeling, young lady?"

"I am feeling – very warm," she assured him with some effort.

"Ah, but we don't want you too warm, do we?" muttered the doctor, feeling her pulse with a frown.

Elvira's head lolled as the doctor examined her and she heard him call over the old woman and bid her give Elvira only warm drinks.

He then went to the door and opened it, letting in a

blast of icy air. Elvira shivered and looked up as the stranger had reappeared alone.

The doctor spoke to the stranger in a low voice before placing a bottle of medicine on the mantelshelf, promising to return next morning to check on his patient.

He put on his cape and departed in another brief frenzy of snow and the old woman bolted the door behind him before shuffling back to her corner.

Elvira shivered again. The stranger frowned and came quickly to adjust the shawl around her shoulders.

She blinked up at him. She did not even know his name. She *must* know his name. Yet that was not the question that rose feebly to her lips.

"Am I – am I – ill?" she murmured.

The stranger looked sombre.

"You have been literally chilled to the bone. We must keep you warm and alert."

He glanced round and took down the medicine bottle and a spoon from the mantelshelf. Shaking it, he poured a little into the spoon and held it to her lips.

Elvira, like a child in her fevered state, turned her face away.

"I don't like the smell."

"You must take it."

"I w-won't."

The stranger regarded her sternly.

"Make no mistake, I will take a whip to you if you continue to refuse."

Elvira looked round eyes widening.

"Y-you would not do such a thing!"

"Would I not!" growled the strange grimly. Without

more ado, he grasped Elvira's chin in his free hand and then levered the spoon between her lips and thus forced, she took a sip.

"All of it," ordered the stranger.

Elvira took a full gulp and swallowed.

"Urgh!"

"Good. In another hour we will repeat the exercise."

"You – you mean to kill me," groaned Elvira.

"No, madam. I mean to cure you."

Elvira turned her head to and fro against the pillow.

"You are cruel. I am sure your Master wouldn't be so cruel to me."

The stranger regarded her, his dark brow ravelled.

"Ah. My Master."

"I do not even k-know his name," complained Elvira. "Or yours."

The stranger gave a thin smile.

"You forget that I do not know yours either, madam. I haven't the least idea who you are."

He paused as Elvira had grown still and was staring up at him. In the dancing firelight she was pale as a wraith, her fevered irises large and the colour of crushed violets. The stranger drew in his breath.

"Perhaps," he said softly, "perhaps you are a sprite, a beautiful winter sprite."

His eyes lingered for a moment on her glistening lips. Then his gaze travelled on and Elvira blushed, mindful that she wore only her bodice. She lifted her hand to draw the shawl over her breast, but was arrested by the sudden flame that flared in the stranger's features.

"So marble white," he muttered. Then, as if to check

himself, he turned abruptly away, throwing himself onto the pew opposite and stared into the fire.

It felt to Elvira as if a searching light had passed from her face, so intent had been his gaze. Her face felt hot with more than fever.

"I should very much – like something to drink," she asked in a faltering voice.

The old woman was fast asleep again and after a glance her way the stranger rose and took a pewter mug. He drew a leather flask from his waistcoat pocket, poured a little of its contents into the mug and added hot water.

Without looking directly at Elvira, he proffered her the mug.

"Drink this. It's warm, as the doctor ordered."

Gratefully, Elvira took the concoction and drank. It coursed with immediate heat through her veins.

The stranger sat back down, resting his elbow on the pew's arm and his forehead on his hand. Still he seemed reluctant to look Elvira's way.

"How long will the storm last, do you think?" asked Elvira tentatively, cradling the cup in her hands.

"You wish to be out of my company so soon?" retorted the stranger dryly.

"Why no. I almost wish – I did not have to leave this place at all, for I have no idea – what manner of welcome I shall receive – at Baseheart."

Slowly the stranger lowered his hand from his face.

"*Baseheart*?" he repeated.

"Y-yes." Elvira's voice almost faded to a whisper. "It has lots of – turrets and – pinnacles. My uncle by marriage lives there and I am to be companion to his daughter – Delphine."

"Delphine." The stranger sat up, staring now with narrowed eyes. "You are well acquainted with her then?"

Elvira shook her head.

"I have not seen her since we were children and then only once."

"Once?" The stranger seemed to marvel. "When you are cousins?"

Elvira lowered her head.

"After my aunt Lady Baseheart died – I was not invited to visit again. Until now."

"Until now – as paid companion," commented the stranger sardonically.

Elvira gave a start.

"Paid? Oh, I don't think I shall be, but I shall be looked after."

The stranger frowned.

"And your parents approve?"

Elvira's eyes misted.

"My parents are dead. They eloped, you know." She passed a hand across her brow. "My father was a poor musician, but he died before I was born and my mother not much later. My mother's other sister brought me up. Aunt Willis."

"Ah," murmured the stranger in wry recognition. "Aunt Willis."

"I am sorry to leave Aunt Willis. She doesn't show affection, but you must not think – that she will not miss me. I am sure she will miss me and I just wish that Delphine – hadn't been so cruel about her."

The stranger leaned forward, elbows on his knees.

"Cruel? Delphine? But you said you had not seen

her for some time."

"I haven't," cried Elvira, "but she sent me a letter and the letter made me think I might not like her."

"What did she say that made you think such a thought?"

"She also said she hoped I was passably pretty because she couldn't bear ugly things. She said her Aunt Cruddock, Lord Baseheart's sister, who lives with them at Baseheart – sometimes made her stomach turn and she said Aunt Willis was a horror and she would like to take the shears to – the hairs on her chin."

"I see."

The stranger turned away, a curious look on his face.

"If she has an aunt who lives with her, why does she need a companion?"

"She wants someone her own age with her – someone who will not be too watchful – when her suitor comes."

The stranger looked round.

"Her suitor?"

"Yes. He's *nearly* a Prince. That is to say, he's the heir to a Prince and she said she will make him her slave."

"Did she indeed?"

Elvira wondered at the rapt way in which the stranger had listened to her for so long as her head sank back against the pillow.

"I have talked so much – about myself," she sighed wearily.

"No, madam. I have tired you with my questions." He took the empty mug from her hand. "Try to rest now. There is a bed in the loft that the old lady earlier assured me is freshly made. Do you think you have recovered your strength enough to climb the ladder?"

"I am not sure." Elvira eyed the ladder doubtfully.

"Try," urged the stranger. "I will aid you."

He slipped an arm about her and helped her up. Together they crossed to the ladder. She set her foot on the lowest rung and paused, feeling faint. His arm gripped her tighter and she instinctively leaned into his strength.

For a moment they stood close, his breath on her neck, the scent of her hair in his nostrils. The room seemed suddenly suspended in time, lit on one side by the flames of the fire, on the other by a shaft of moonlight that filtered through the leaded window.

"The moonlight is bright," Elvira murmured.

"Yes." The stranger's voice stirred her hair. "The snowstorm has ceased. The sky is now clear and the moon full. You will be able to journey on tomorrow."

"To Baseheart," sighed Elvira.

"To Baseheart. Yes." The stranger's voice was deep and soft.

Still they stood as if enraptured. A faint snore sounded from the old woman and a log in the fire fell to ashes.

"You must go up," he muttered at last.

Almost reluctantly, Elvira released herself from his clasp and began to mount the ladder. The hem of her petticoat impeded her and at last she caught it up, all too aware that this now exposed her ankles to the stranger's gaze. She was relieved to sense him turn his head away.

She reached the trap door and pushed it open. With one last effort, she pulled herself up.

The loft smelt of hay and apples and gratefully she

crawled towards the pallet that lay under a small window.

The stranger's head appeared in the aperture.

"I forgot. You must take this."

He pushed across the medicine bottle and spoon and Elvira stared at it dully.

"Must I?"

"Yes. It has already helped you."

Elvira reached for the bottle and poured out a spoonful and swallowed it under the stranger's eye.

"Good," he said with a smile. "I would not, after all, have you expire on my watch!"

Next he was gone, she heard him descend and imagined him setting himself down by the fire.

She lay back staring up at frosty stars. He had rescued her from the snow, threatened her with a beating, forced her to take medicine, listened to her rambling on about Baseheart and Delphine – and she still did not know his name.

'I must find out tomorrow,' she promised herself.

She drew the old woman's quilt up to her chin and gave a sigh. She was drifting into sleep when she became aware of footsteps from the room below. She opened her eyes and listened.

Someone was pacing the room from corner to corner. It must be the stranger.

Obviously trying not to wake the old woman, his footfall was stealthy, yet to Elvira the sound was like the beating of a dark and troubled heart.

CHAPTER THREE

The sun was bright and birds were singing. Elvira breathed on the glass of the loft window until a hole formed in the ice and she could just see an edge of white thatch.

She sat back on her heels listening. From below she heard the smack of clogs on the stone floor, which must be the old woman.

There was no sound indicating the presence of the stranger.

Remembering herself clasped against his bosom the night before, a faint flush suffused her cheeks. She had not been herself – she had been in a fever – the concoction he gave her had gone to her head!

She buried her face in her hands mortified. It would be best if she never saw him again. Perhaps, she thought hopefully, he and his Master have already departed!

She raised her head as the smell of hot milk and fresh bread came wafting up through the rafters. She was very hungry.

She must go down and eat or skulk in the loft and die of starvation.

She ran her fingers through her tousled hair, threw her shawl over her crumpled shift and pushed back the trap door.

The old woman looked up as Elvira descended the ladder. She pointed at a table laid with a gingham cloth and set with dishes.

"There be breakfast," she croaked.

All thoughts of the stranger disappeared at the sight of food as Elvira fell greedily upon the bread and honey. She ate three slices and drank two mugs of hot milk before she felt sated.

She felt so much better and wondered at her frail state the night before.

She looked round. The old woman was sitting on the pew, hands folded in her lap, eyes half closed.

"What time of day is it?"

The old woman glanced toward the window as if the patch of sky beyond was her clock.

"Near enough ten of the hour," she said.

Elvira was astonished that she had slept so long. She hesitated to ask her next question, but ask it she must.

"W-where is – everybody?"

"You mean the gentleman as brought you 'ere," asked the old woman disconcertingly. "He be gone with the other fellow."

Elvira supposed that 'the other fellow' referred to the stranger's Master.

"W-where have they gone?"

"To change the 'orses, but it must be done already, for 'ere be the carriage."

Elvira turned her head and sure enough, the Baseheart carriage was drawing up before the window. At the same moment a rap at the door announced the doctor.

He came in, his face rosy from the cold air and placed his black bag on a chair.

"Seems I'm just in time," he said, indicating the carriage. "My patient is about to be whisked away."

"I don't feel like a patient this morning," responded Elvira politely.

"You don't look like one, either," returned the doctor cheerfully. He felt for her pulse and after a few moments gave a satisfied grunt. "Hmn! Fit to travel, young lady. Either my medicine is better than I thought or there's been some magic afoot."

"M-magic?" echoed Elvira faintly, thinking of the devoted attentions of the stranger and the warmth of his arms about her waist. But the doctor had turned away and was picking up his black bag.

"I am not needed here," he announced.

Elvira rose in a sudden panic.

"But sir – I must pay you."

"Pay me?" The doctor shook his head. "No need. The young man paid me already."

"H-he paid?"

"He did indeed." The doctor glanced down and pursed his lips. "You have made a remarkable recovery, young lady, but I do suggest you put on your boots now."

Elvira stared down at her bare feet.

"I hadn't noticed."

"Ah, youth!" the doctor smiled. "Well good-day to you now miss. Good-day, ma'am."

This latter adieu was to the old woman, who nodded amiably from her pew. The doctor departed, encountering the carriage driver on the threshold.

Elvira scurried over to the hearth to put on her boots. She splashed her face with water and then with great effort fixed up her hair and the old woman helped her into her skirt, blouse and cape.

The clothes were all dry, but felt rather stiff and cold and Elvira regretted the horse blanket that had blown away in the wind. The journey was sure to be chilly and the thought made her shiver. The next moment the old woman tapped her on the arm.

"This were left for your use," she said, holding out the stranger's dark cloak.

Elvira took it in a daze and as she draped it around her shoulders it seemed still to retain the warmth of the stranger within its folds.

She would have liked to remunerate the old woman for her hospitality, but she shook her head. The gentleman had given her a piece of silver.

Elvira felt faint at the thought of how increasingly indebted she was to this man whose name was a mystery to her!

When she stepped outside she blinked in the bright sun and stared at the carriage. The two lacklustre horses of the day before had gone. In the shafts now were two glossy chestnuts with bright eyes.

"What happened to yesterday's horses?" she asked the driver, hoping that the poor creatures had at least survived the night.

"They were exhausted after their ordeal," he replied. "Those two fellows brought new 'orses and took the others away. They'll leave them at an 'ostelry in Gloucester for me to collect when they've rested."

"So the gentlemen were going on to Gloucester?"

"That's what the one who spent the night 'ere at the cottage told me," replied the driver. "The other one – the one who went for the doctor and then 'elped me and the lads dig out the carriage – he barely opened his mouth. Spoke no English."

"Spoke no English?" repeated Elvira amazed.

That probably explained why it was the servant who had remained with her and not the Master, who would not have been able to converse with her. She wondered how he had fared with the doctor and then remembered that he had been furnished with a note.

Still it was strange to think of the Master doing the work of the servant and the servant acting the part of the Master.

'Would the Master have held me so close, breathed so sweetly upon my neck?'

The question rushed so unbidden into her mind that Elvira was shocked.

The sooner she was away from the scene of her encounter with the stranger, the better.

She climbed quickly into the carriage, neither expecting nor receiving the help of the driver. She was just reaching to close the door when a voice assailed her.

"Would you leave without bidding me farewell?"

It was the stranger, seemingly appearing out of nowhere. He was standing in front of the cottage, holding a black stallion by the reins.

"I – thought you had already departed."

The stranger looped the reins of his horse around a tree and came forward.

"I could not depart without assuring myself that you had fully recovered."

"I have recovered, as you can see." Elvira averted her eyes. "Thanks in no small part to your ministrations. I am deeply indebted to you – not least for your cloak! I cannot think how I may ever repay you when I do not even know your name."

The stranger rested his hand on the carriage door.

"The pleasure of having been of service is payment enough. But my name, since you request it so charmingly – is Serge."

Elvira raised her eyes to him and encountered his unblinking gaze.

"S-Serge?"

"That is right. And now madam, what name am I to remember you by?"

"It is Elvira," she told him in a near whisper. "Elvira Carrisford."

"Elvira!" murmured Serge. "Well, Miss Elvira, it is in the stars that we shall meet again."

Elvira raised her eyes in alarm, but the stranger was already closing the door.

"Your Master. What is *his* name?" she called.

Too late!

Stepping back, Serge signalled to the driver and the carriage was off. Elvira leaned forward and tried to catch a last glimpse of him, but he was lost to view.

She sank back, burying herself in Serge's cloak.

"*It's in the stars that we shall meet again.*"

What had he meant? Was he just teasing her?

An image rose in her mind.

The wench at the *White Doe Inn* sauntering so casually across to the stranger – Serge – where he leaned against the post. And then later, waiting for him with a towel over her arm. This Serge was used to the attention of women and he was well able to play upon their susceptibilities.

And she, Elvira, had been the most susceptible of all, unused as she was to the company of the opposite sex.

Aunt Willis would not have approved!

At the thought of Aunt Willis, a pang shot through Elvira's heart. She doubted that she would ever see the stern old lady again.

Well, Aunt Willis and the adventure of the snowstorm and Serge and the cottage – all this was behind her now. Her future lay ahead, on the other side of the forest, beneath the pinnacles and turrets of Baseheart Castle –

*

Though the cloak kept her body warm, Elvira's feet grew chill. She stamped them to try and keep them warm and even took off her boots to rub her toes, but her hands were not much warmer.

She was relieved when at last the carriage rolled in through the gates of the Baseheart Estate.

It was late afternoon and there was a bluish hue to the air. Elvira wound down the window and leaned out, staring ahead in anticipation.

When she had been left alone in the snow-bound carriage – only last night, though it seemed eons ago now – she had pictured the castle as frozen, under a spell and with spires of ice. Now, as it hove into view, she gasped to see how closely it resembled her conjured image.

Icicles hung from battlements, windowsills and spires. Frozen ivy clung like a shroud to the massive walls and the myriad windows looked white and lifeless. Turrets disappeared into what seemed like low cloud.

The carriage halted before wide stone steps that led up to a nail-studded main door. No one appeared to welcome her.

Silence reigned.

Elvira could hear the jingling of the horses' harness and the sound of the driver cursing under his breath. A rook landed on one of the balustrades and cawed angrily at the intruders.

Elvira decided she must get out and ring the brass bell. She swung her door open and stepped down, eyes immediately smarting in the cold air.

She stared up at her new home.

Perhaps the castle was indeed under a spell, its inhabitants asleep for a thousand years!

She was about to mount the steps when the main door creaked wide and a woman in a housekeeper's cap and apron stepped out. She flapped her apron at the rook before calling down to Elvira.

"Miss Carrisford?"

Elvira nodded, trying to stop her teeth chattering.

"I am the housekeeper, Mrs. Prendergast. You poor thing, you look frozen! Do come in."

The rook flew about Elvira's head as she mounted the steps. At the top she turned to wave farewell to the driver, but he had climbed down from his box and was already untying the ropes that held her trunk.

Mrs. Prendergast ushered Elvira into the Great Hall with tapestries on the walls and a spacious mahogany staircase. In a marble hearth logs the size of small trees crackled and spat.

Elvira held her hands out to the flames while Mrs. Prendergast summoned a footman and two servants to fetch the luggage.

"The household is all behind today," she explained to Elvira. "The family were at a ball and almost didn't make it back in the blizzard. That's why they weren't down to greet you. At this rate, they probably won't be up until lunchtime."

"Not true, Prendergast!" a voice called out from above. "I'm up now!"

Elvira, hands still on the fire, turned and her eyes widened at the creature who stood at the top of the staircase.

It was Delphine, but quite different to the shy little girl with flowing locks she remembered. For one thing, the flowing locks were now arranged in an elaborate display of ringlets, feathers and combs. This despite the fact that Delphine was still in her dressing gown, admittedly a lavish affair of velvet and ermine.

And the expression on her face was far from shy.

"Miss Delphine," scolded Mrs. Prendergast, "you are not properly dressed."

"Oh, phooey, Prendergast, it's only my cousin!"

This remark was followed with a giggle as Delphine came running down the stairs, silver bracelets jangling on her plump forearm.

She arrived before Elvira and stood surveying her, head on one side.

"Well," she pronounced finally. "You aren't ugly anyhow."

"Neither are you, cousin," responded Elvira politely.

"Oh, I am the local beauty, don't you know," pouted

Delphine airily. "You being the least bit pretty doesn't worry me one bit. But we were expecting you yesterday. We were due to go to a ball and when you didn't arrive by dusk we decided to go anyway. Prendergast was here to welcome you, after all."

"Miss Delphine," intervened Mrs. Prendergast with insistence. "The servants will be here any moment. You cannot be seen in your dressing gown."

Delphine gave a nonchalant shrug and turned away.

"Come on, cousin. I'll take you to your room. My aunt and I chose it for you."

Without another word to the housekeeper, Delphine seized Elvira's hand.

"Don't you take any notice of that Prendergast," she advised as she led her up the stairs. "Papa only puts up with her because she's been here since he was a boy. And I'm only in my dressing gown because Cissie my maid had just finished my hair when I heard the carriage and I was so impatient to see you!

"Papa says I'm a free spirit and it doesn't matter that I never had a governess as my aunt Cruddock taught me to read and write and anyway beautiful people don't have to bother with such things.

"I am to marry the nephew of a Prince after all and he's not interested in whether I can write sums or recite poetry. He's seen my miniature and he's interested in my translucent skin and hazel eyes and whether I can sing like a bird which I can and dance which I can. I really am a very good catch for a Prince, don't you know."

The chatter continued and soon Elvira became dazed and was barely listening. She felt herself propelled through a number of wide corridors, passing sombre portraits, gilt chairs and leaded windows. Up yet another stairway, along an uncarpeted corridor and Delphine triumphantly threw open a door.

"Here!" she announced.

Elvira stepped in and looked round.

A worsted curtain hung at the tiny window and a plain brown quilt was draped over a high bed. Next to a dilapidated armoire a jug and basin stood on a marble-topped table.

Her bedroom at Aunt Willis's had looked more welcoming than this, but she resolutely would not allow herself to be downcast. After all, there was a log fire burning merrily in the grate and the room was far enough from the household to guarantee a degree of privacy.

It also contained an object that Aunt Willis would never have countenanced and this was a mahogany pier glass, its mirror hidden under a large dust sheet.

Delpine leapt on the bed and sat on the edge, swinging her legs.

"Lady Cruddock said we shouldn't choose too grand a room. You are just a *companion,* you know."

"I am perfectly happy with this, I assure you," said Elvira, eyeing the pier glass with interest as she untied her bonnet.

"Oh," responded Delphine in a tone that suggested she might have enjoyed a little dissension. "That's all right then."

Two footmen now carried in her trunk, while a third brought in her two carpet bags and Serge's cloak.

Elvira took the cloak and held it for a moment, crumpled against her breast.

Once the servants had departed she placed the cloak on a chair by the fireplace and went over to her trunk.

Taking a key from her pocket, she knelt to unlock it.

Delphine exclaimed in horror.

"You're surely not planning to unpack yourself? Send for your maid immediately!"

"I prefer to do it," replied Elvira stiffly.

She didn't like to admit that she was not used to the services of a personal maid. At Aunt Willis's there had been a cook and a general housemaid and that was all.

"Well!" sniffed Delphine. "If you must." She peered curiously over Elvira's shoulder as she drew out her gowns. "That blue is hardly suitable for a companion. You need more sombre colours to distinguish you from *me,* don't you know! I have to be quite distinctive when the Prince's nephew arrives."

"They are all I have," sighed Elvira, glancing at Delphine's violent green taffeta with its plaid collar and thinking her quite distinctive enough.

A gong sounded far below and Delphine slid quickly off the bed.

"I must go and dress. That's lunch."

Elvira, tired after the journey and her cousin's verbal onslaught, felt herself quail.

"Would you object, cousin," she ventured, "if I did not attend lunch? I should like to rest before meeting your father – and Lady Cruddock."

She was expecting a petulant outburst, but to her astonishment Delphine turned on a gaze of quite sincere concern.

"Oh, you poor creature, *of course* you must rest. I've chattered on, haven't I? I just don't think sometimes, Papa says so. I shall make your excuses and I am sure they will understand. You must attend supper, though!"

"I w-will," murmured Elvira, wondering at the sudden temperature change in her cousin.

Delphine disappeared with a wave of her hand. Elvira listened to her footsteps patter away down the corridor and then she began to unbutton her blouse. She slipped gratefully out of her skirt and her eyes alighted again on the pier glass.

She tugged at the dust sheet and stepped back as it slithered to the floor.

She stared quizzically at her reflection in the shimmering mirror.

Was it possible, as the stranger had said, that she possessed beauty? Singular charms? Was her breast – and here Elvira's hand strayed to the area of flesh now visible above the line of her corset – was her breast truly *marble white*?

'*I am not ugly at least*,' she decided with a sudden giggle.

Taking Serge's cloak from the chair, she moved over to the bed and sank gratefully down. The cloak was her quilt. She would rest for half-an-hour before she would set about unpacking.

She was aroused some time later by the sound of a rattling coalscuttle. She lifted her head to see her maid bob up shyly from the hearth.

"Shall I bring you some hot water, miss?" she asked. "Supper is at six o'clock sharp."

"Thank you, yes please," said Elvira, glancing at the window. It was quite dark outside. She must have slept most of the afternoon!

When the maid returned with a jug of hot water and warm towels, Elvira washed herself at the marble-topped table. The maid, whose name, she discovered, was Beth, helped her into her best dress and then attended to her hair.

"There's hardly anything to hold it up, miss. Do you have any more pins?"

"None," replied Elvira ruefully, remembering the way the wind had snatched the pins from her head the day before. "But there's a ribbon in my trunk."

In her blue dress, her hair arranged prettily behind her, Elvira took one last look at herself in the pier glass.

"I am rather too pale," she commented critically.

"Pinch your cheeks, miss," advised Beth.

"Thank you, I will."

Cheeks a little pinker, Elvira descended nervously to the dining room.

Her uncle had been such a remote figure when she had visited with Aunt Willis all those years ago that her knees began to tremble as she crossed the carpet to greet him. She barely took in the figure of Lady Cruddock standing in the shadows.

Lord Baseheart regarded Elvira from under bushy brows as she rose from her curtsy.

"Dashed good looks," he muttered, not altogether pleasantly. "Eh, sister?"

Lady Cruddock, bristling in black satin widow's weeds, moved forward. She was stout with a distinctly malicious eye.

"You may have made a mistake in bringing her here, brother," she remarked. "She puts your daughter in the shade."

"Oh, that's impossible," blurted out Elvira in shock. "I have never – hardly ever – attracted the least attention."

Lord Baseheart scowled.

"Most disingenuous! But did you mark that '*hardly ever*', sister? I'd say she was alluding to her recent encounter on the forest road."

Elvira's heart skipped a beat.

"E-encounter?" she stammered.

"Don't play the innocent with us, young lady," snapped Lady Cruddock. "The driver told us all."

"W-what 'all' is there to tell?" asked Elvira.

Lord Baseheart glowered.

"You were caught in a blizzard. A young gentleman, who it seems never divulged his name, at least to our driver, rescued you. The two of you then passed the night alone in a cottage."

"Not alone!" exclaimed Elvira indignantly. "There was an old woman there."

"Pshaw!" Lord Baseheart gestured dismissively. "Deaf and dumb and half-witted, no doubt."

"Turn a blind eye for a shilling, I shouldn't wonder," put in Lady Cruddock.

"No, *no*. She only – fell asleep for a time." Elvira wrung her hands.

Lord Baseheart and his sister exchanged a glance.

"Can you then assure me, niece," demanded Lord Baseheart, "that no improprieties occurred?"

"None!" cried Elvira, in so heartfelt a manner that they seemed satisfied.

"We shall let the matter rest for now," said Lord Baseheart, "but let me warn you – you are never to recount your recent misadventure to your cousin. My daughter is of a singularly innocent and impressionable nature."

"I s-shall say nothing."

"Good." Lord Baseheart looked her up and down. "I hope you understand you are subordinate to Delphine in everything and that includes your dress. This sapphire blue is too ostentatious. I shall ask my sister to provide you with more suitable attire."

"I'll consider it a duty," added Lady Cruddock grimly. "We can't have her drawing the eye when Charles Rowland arrives."

"Indeed not," agreed Lord Baseheart. "But hush now, for here's Delphine."

His whole manner and demeanour changed as he greeted his daughter. He cast her a look of such doting indulgence that Elvira felt an unaccustomed pang of envy. No one had ever looked at her like that.

"What a picture," murmured Lord Baseheart, leading Delphine to the table.

Delphine was dressed in yellow silk with diamonds glittering on her breast. She had powdered her face and reddened her lips and looked overly sophisticated for her age.

"Elvira is quite jealous," observed Lady Cruddock with satisfaction.

Lord Baseheart and Delphine laughed while, as if in compliance, a rook gave a malicious caw outside the window.

Elvira lowered her head.

There surely could not have been a less auspicious start to her new life at Baseheart Castle!

CHAPTER FOUR

The window of Elvira's room must have been closed for some time for the latch was stiff and it took all her efforts to push it open.

More snow had fallen during the night and trees and hedges were mantled. The sky looked dour and grey with a wan sun struggling to shine.

A figure on horseback came into view on the road from the gates. Covered in a voluminous cloak, it was hard to distinguish whether it was a man or a woman and Elvira watched until the figure disappeared from view.

A moment later there came the faint trill of the castle bell and Elvira wondered who this visitor might be.

She withdrew from the window as Beth entered bearing a dress over her arm.

"Lady Cruddock said I was to bring this to you, miss."

The dress was dun-coloured serge. Elvira's heart sank but she gave Beth a determinedly cheerful smile.

"That will be most practical," she commented.

"Practical if you was to peel apples in the kitchen or sweep the stairs," replied Beth, who felt aggrieved on behalf of her new Mistress.

"I am sure it is practical for a companion too," declared Elvira firmly.

Silently Beth helped her don the offending garment. Elvira thought it better to resist surveying herself in the pier glass. Leaving her hair loose over her shoulders, she was about to turn for the door when Beth restrained her.

"Wait, miss," she urged, fumbling in her apron pocket. "I've brought a clasp for you."

Elvira's eyes widened as Beth held out the clasp.

"But Beth – it's tortoiseshell – isn't that rather luxurious?"

"You mean for a lady's maid to have acquired?"

"Oh, Beth no!" Elvira was mortified. "I meant, for *me*!"

Beth softened.

"My last Mistress gave it to me before I left. She was very fond of me, but I've no occasion to wear it."

"I would hardly call breakfast with the Basehearts an occasion, Beth," said Elvira, eyeing the clasp ruefully.

"Oh, don't you worry. Miss Delphine will be ornamented for a ball! Why shouldn't you have something a little showy for yourself? Here, let me just pull back your hair and fix it for you."

Convinced and not entirely against her will, Elvira bent her head. Beth secured the clasp and stood back to admire her handiwork.

"There, miss, it's you what's fit for a Prince now!"

Beth was reckless and partisan, but she made Elvira feel a little less neglected.

Lady Cruddock was alone at the breakfast table and she gave an approving nod at the dun-coloured dress.

A footman pulled out a chair for Elvira and a serving maid hurried forward with a plate of kedgeree.

"Is Delphine – not joining us?" she asked.

"Oh, for Heaven's sake don't wait for Delphine or your food will be stone cold," replied Lady Cruddock. "I don't know how any girl could take so long over her *toilette*. She won't be down for another half-hour or so, I'll warrant."

"And L-Lord Baseheart?" enquired Elvira further, rather hoping she was to be spared his unyielding presence that morning.

"He always breakfasts alone in his room, although he was disturbed this morning by a messenger."

Elvira remembered the figure arriving on horseback. She asked no more questions, however, and began eating.

As she pushed her dish away, Delphine bounced in dressed in lime-coloured silk with an array of bracelets clattering on her wrists.

"Cousin!" she called, eyeing Elvira up and down. "You certainly look the part now."

"Doesn't she, though," agreed Lady Cruddock with satisfaction.

Delphine circled behind Elvira's chair.

"That's a rather expensive clasp in your hair. Surely not a present from Aunt Willis?"

"No – " replied Elvira, thankful to be saved further elaboration by the entrance of Lord Baseheart, who burst through the door with a letter in his hand.

"What is it, Papa?" cried Delphine.

Lord Baseheart leaned a hand on the table, breathing heavily as if he had just run down the stairs.

"From Charles Rowland," he puffed, waving the letter. "There's been a development."

"Development?" Delphine looked bewildered.

"Rowland was on his way here when a messenger intercepted his journey to inform him that his uncle had died. He has returned to France immediately to attend to the funeral and to claim his inheritance." He took a deep breath. "Rowland is now *Prince Charles de Courel*."

Delphine sank onto a chair.

"I won't have to wait then – to be a Princess!"

Lady Cruddock, who had been listening intently, pursed her lips.

"Don't you forget that Charles Rowland was only considering the marriage in order to please his uncle and secure his future title. The old Prince's death has relieved him of that obligation and you may no longer have a suitor at all."

Delphine gave out a terrible wail.

"*Papa*! Say it isn't true."

"Now don't you fret, my darling," Lord Baseheart soothed her, shooting an angry glance at Lady Cruddock, "it isn't true at all."

"There!" trumpeted Delphine to Elvira, as if it was her who had uttered the dire warning.

"Rowland – Prince Charles de Courel – has informed me that he wishes to honour his late uncle's wishes," continued Lord Baseheart, "and as soon as he has settled affairs in France he will return to meet you."

Delphine snatched the letter from her father's hand and perused it greedily.

"Why, he was almost here when he turned back!" she moaned. "I don't see why he couldn't have continued on to Baseheart, proposed to me properly and *then* returned to France for the funeral."

"Perhaps he felt too sad. He must, after all, have been very fond of his uncle," suggested Elvira.

"Fond? Fiddlesticks!" scorned Delphine. "I hope, cousin, you are not thinking to *reprimand* me in any way?"

"I would not dream of doing so," responded Elvira, looking down.

"I should think not," scolded Lord Baseheart. "Delphine is beyond reproach in every way. You would do well to profit by her example of well-bred behaviour."

"Yes, Lord Baseheart."

Elvira bit her lip. She was beginning to realise that the best policy with the Baseheart family was to agree with everything or say nothing.

Returning thankfully to her room she discovered that Lady Cruddock had ordered her three blue dresses removed from the armoire. In their place were three dresses as plain and unappealing as the dun-coloured one. There was a sage green, a mustard and a dark brown.

With a sudden ferocity, Elvira picked up the dustsheet and threw it over the pier glass.

For many years she had existed without ever seeing herself clearly and at full length. One look in the pier glass had encouraged her to believe that she might just be as – as appealing as the stranger, Serge, had suggested.

But her confidence was fading as even if it was true, what good would it do? Dressed in thick dresses of sombre colour, no rice powder for her cheeks, no vermilion for her lips, no fan, no kid gloves – who would ever notice her?

Not even the clerk her Aunt Willis had so fondly imagined as her suitor. And *never*, in a thousand years, a Prince!

'Even Serge would not extol my beauty now,' she thought ruefully.

*

During the days that followed, Elvira found herself becoming increasingly despondent.

If Delphine did not desire her presence she was left with nothing constructive to do but wander the echoing corridors of the vast and gloomy castle with nothing beyond the windows but a silent and white world.

Her feeling of isolation was further compounded by the fact that she seemed to be an object of prurient interest to any servant she encountered. They cast pitying glances her way and she often heard whispers or giggling after she had passed. She felt they dared to do this because they believed her status to be almost as lowly as theirs.

After one too many such occasions Elvira flew to her room in tears, where Beth looked up in astonishment from her mending.

"Why, whatever's ailing you, miss?"

Elvira wiped her tears away quickly with the back of her hand.

"N-nothing, Beth."

"Don't you 'nothing Beth' me, miss!" scolded the maid. "Something or someone's upset you and there's no mistake."

Elvira hung her head.

"Beth – everyone I meet seems to seems to regard me with incivility. Is there – is there some story about me in the servants quarters that I should know about?"

Beth looked away embarrassed.

"Well, miss, as a matter of fact, there is. And it's not savoury. Not that I believe it for one moment and I've said so many a time. But there's some as thrives on gossip and innuendo."

"W-what is the gossip exactly?"

"That you was abducted on the road to Baseheart by a servant and that you passed a night alone in a cottage with him."

Elvira took a deep breath.

"I was rescued, Beth, from perishing alone in a snowstorm. And my rescuer and I were not alone in the cottage. There was an old lady there as well, I swear on the soul of my dear dead mother that this is the truth. Whoever says otherwise is a liar!"

"I knew it!" cried Beth triumphantly. "It was the carriage driver who spread the lie. But I'll hobble *him* next time he opens his mouth. Now you cheer up, miss. I'll stoke up the fire and bring you a mug of hot chocolate."

Beth's kind words raised Elvira's spirits a little.

Whether or not Beth successfully intervened below stairs Elvira never knew, but the looks and the whispers ceased. She might then have experienced a measure of peace but for her uncertain relations with her cousin.

Delphine's humour was so unreliable as to make it impossible to know what to expect. Affable and considerate in the morning, she could be sulky and indifferent in the afternoon.

One minute she treated Elvira as a friend and confidante, the next as a mere servant. She was as capable of clasping Elvira to her bosom and calling her dear cousin as she was of coldly informing her she was in every way an inferior.

Elvira, in a rare moment of indiscretion, described Delphine's behaviour in a letter to her Aunt Willis, who usually replied to her niece's letters tersely, but on this occasion she dedicated much ink and energy in her desire to put Elvira properly in her place.

"*It seems to me that you are not accommodating yourself adequately to your new situation. Despite the blood connection you are in no way Miss Baseheart's equal and you should not expect to be so treated. Whatever her lack of merits, she is your social superior so count yourself lucky that Lord Baseheart has offered you this opportunity to observe your betters at close hand.*

Perhaps you may profit from such proximity. At any rate, our paths have now irrevocably diverged. I shall continue to correspond with you should you so wish, but I certainly do not encourage such sentiments of self-pity and envy as were expressed in your last letter to me."

Elvira, reading the letter before her fire, sat back and stared at the flames.

She had to admit that she had fallen prey to a degree of self-pity these last few days, but *envy*? Of Delphine? Did she want to be Delphine, have what Delphine had? She would *not* have wished Lord Baseheart as her father, that was certain.

She folded the letter sadly. It was now absolutely clear she would never, *could* never, return to her aunt's house and there was no sanctuary for her anywhere.

There was only Baseheart.

With this in mind she applied herself more resolutely to her new role.

The days passed in card games, walks about the wintry garden and reading aloud to her cousin. She was never asked to accompany Delphine on shopping trips or visits to neighbours, but she learned to relish these periods of solitude.

She was all but silent in the presence of Lord Baseheart and his sister and after a while an uneasy truce was established between herself and her hosts.

*

Then word came that Prince Charles de Courel was on his way!

The castle sprang to life.

Suppers, balls and hunting parties were organised.

Lord Baseheart sent for local merchants and arranged for crates of champagne and boxes of cigars to be delivered. Orders were sent out to the estate for a grand slaughter of hogs and cattle, chickens and geese.

Lady Cruddock meanwhile decided that she and Delphine should take the carriage to Gloucester to purchase a trousseau.

Beth, sewing one afternoon while Elvira read, could not refrain from commenting on this venture,

"Trousseau, pah! If you ask me, it's what people call jumping the gun! The Prince hasn't yet set eyes on Miss Delphine, let alone proposed to her."

Elvira looked up from her book.

"But – there's an understanding, isn't there?"

"An *understanding* isn't the same as being fixed in stone," grunted Beth. "This Prince is prepared to carry out his uncle's late wishes, but he's no longer *compelled.*

"If he doesn't like what he sees or hears of your

cousin, he'll smoke Lord Baseheart's cigars, dine on his trout, guzzle his brandy, then pack up his bags and go. Back to his French estates, where he might find himself a pretty little French wife."

Beth bit off a length of thread with satisfaction.

"I hope, for my cousin's sake," frowned Elvira, "that you are wrong. I should not like to see Delphine so disappointed."

Beth glanced at her Mistress slyly.

"What would you say, Miss Elvira, if it was *you* who took the Prince's fancy?"

Elvira regarded Beth sternly.

"It would be wrong of me to even entertain such a notion, Beth, and you must not entertain it on my behalf, even in jest!"

Beth gave a shrug and folded up her sewing.

"If you ask me, you're more fit for a Prince than Miss Delphine," she muttered to herself, but so quietly that Elvira did not hear.

*

Delphine returned from her shopping trip and insisted that Elvira come and inspect her purchases, which lay amid tissue and upturned boxes on her bed.

Elvira circled the bed in wonder. She had never seen such an array of finery. Satin gowns, embroidered silk blouses, silk shifts, fur stoles, delicate Chinese slippers, not to mention trays of glittering jewellery.

She picked up a rose-coloured evening gown and examined it. Tiny pearls were sewn on pale net over the skirt.

"Try it on," Delphine urged her.

Elvira hesitated.

"I want you to," ordered Delphine as she clicked her fingers at her maid. "Cassie, help Miss Elvira out of her dress."

Cassie cast a disapproving look, but obviously did not dare countermand her.

"I do not – think this is right," protested Elvira, uncomfortably aware of Cassie's expression.

"Oh, shush!" said Delphine with a light tap on her cousin's arm. "You're not to vex me. You are to be my mannequin and there's an end of it!"

Elvira submitted to her cousin's humour, allowing Cassie to help her on with the evening gown.

She raised her eyes to Delphine's mirror and stared.

The rose colour of the gown emphasised the rose of her complexion. What would Serge have said had he seen her dressed like this?

Delphine grunted approvingly. Searching among the items of clothing she finally picked up an ermine cape and draped it over Elvira's shoulders. The effect of the pure white fur against her delicate skin and auburn hair was startling.

She surveyed her, head on one side, chewing her lower lip.

Elvira meanwhile was overcome with the sensation of the soft fur against her cheek. It was so deliciously soft! She could have worn it forever!

"It needs – something else," Delphine was musing.

She stretched out and took an emerald necklace from a tray. Lifting Elvira's hair at the nape, she placed the piece of jewellery around her neck.

"How very interesting!" came Lady Cruddock's

voice at the door.

Delphine turned.

"Interesting? What do you mean, aunt?"

Elvira, watching Lady Cruddock closely in the mirror, thought she detected an expression of pure mischief in her eyes.

"I mean," sighed Lady Cruddock, "that here is a perfect illustration of the maxim that clothes maketh the man, or in this case, woman. Elvira looks quite the little Princess."

Delphine looked worriedly at Elvira.

"*Princess*?"

"Yes. It's probably a good thing she is not to attend any of the events taking place during the Prince's visit. You might find you have a rival."

Delphine's jaw trembled. She snatched at the fur cape around Elvira's shoulders.

"Take it off! Take everything off!"

A flicker at the edge of Lady Cruddock's lips betrayed satisfaction at the emotions she had aroused.

"Now, now, niece," she purred consolingly. "I only jest. The clothes look well on Elvira, but they will look immeasurably better on *you.* You are a pure blood, after all – she is *not*."

Delphine visibly relaxed.

"You are right, aunt. I *am* a pure blood and I look it, don't I? I look it even without the gown and the cape and the necklace. Even without all that, I'm enchanting and aristocratic, aren't I?"

"Indeed you are," agreed Lady Cruddock. "And furthermore, you must remember that the Prince is interested in marrying the daughter of a Baseheart, not the daughter of an obscure *Carrisford*."

Elvira quite forgot her resolution not to cross a Baseheart in any way.

"I am proud to be my father's daughter," she burst out. "He – may not have been *born* noble, but he had a noble heart."

"Your sentiments do you credit," responded Lady Cruddock with a tight smile. "But they do not elevate your position in this household or any other."

"That's right," endorsed Delphine. "And now I'm getting bored with seeing you in those clothes. So take them off and we'll go and play a game of whist!"

Biting back her anger and sense of humiliation, Elvira complied. She stepped out of the dress as it dropped to the floor and stoically refrained from kicking it aside.

'Aunt Willis's training is standing me in good stead,' she thought with a degree of bitterness. 'No one can argue that I do not know my place now.'

It was not just the Calvinistic principles of her aunt that were now guiding Elvira's behaviour. It was also an innate pride that refused to allow her to reveal how hurt or affected she was by the treatment meted out to her.

One day she might find a way to be free of this household, but for now she was as good as prisoner here.

*

The great day at last arrived.

The whole household assembled in the Great Hall to greet the illustrious visitor. The housemaids were all in freshly starched aprons and the footmen smelt of pomade. Even Elvira was expected to attend and indeed Lady

Cruddock sent her a yellow ribbon to wear with her mustard-coloured dress.

All morning Delphine fluttered and fussed before her mirror.

"How do I look, Elvira? Do I look ravishing? *I* think I look ravishing."

Delphine was in turquoise. The net of her gown was voluminous and seemed to froth about her body.

"You look – quite singular, Delphine," answered Elvira with great circumspection.

Delphine, eminently pleased with herself, was in an expansive mood.

"And you look splendid, cousin," she announced.

Elvira thanked her politely. She was sure she knew exactly how she looked in her mustard-coloured dress, her hair tied with a small yellow ribbon

Plain as a pikestaff!

Cassie appeared at the door.

"The carriage has just been seen at the head of the drive."

Delphine trembled with excitement.

"Elvira – just fluff up my train, will you? Oh, I think I've never looked so – so – *comme il faut*!"

The two cousins descended just in time.

The carriage had drawn up outside and Delphine hastened to her father, who took her hand and kissed it.

Elvira placed herself behind the line of servants and was beginning to thrill with anticipation herself. After all she had never set eyes on a real Prince before!

A murmur ran through the gathering as a footman stepped up to the front door. He opened it wide and Prince

Charles de Courel entered with his valet.

The footman standing in front of Elvira was tall, so she edged sideways, but still she could not see the Prince.

Raising herself on tiptoe, her eyes settled instead on the valet and immediately widened in shock.

It was the stranger! The very stranger she had encountered at the *White Doe Inn*. The stranger who had rescued her from the storm. The stranger whose name she had finally learned was Serge.

In that case, the 'Master' she had never seen – the 'Master' who had gone to fetch the doctor and who had helped to repair the carriage – was the very same Prince who now stood in the hall.

Elvira felt faint as she thought of the time she had spent with Serge at the cottage.

Why, oh, why had she confessed to him her reservations about the character of the cousin she had not seen for so long? The cousin who was the fiancée of his Master? Supposing – and now Elvira began to blush guiltily – supposing Serge had repeated those reservations to the Prince? Supposing the Prince had returned to meet Delphine with her indiscretions planted in his mind?

Elvira could not bear to think that she might prove the instrument that blighted her cousin's romantic dreams.

She must see the Prince's face as he was introduced to Delphine.

Elvira moved to the left of the footman and her eyes found the Prince.

In an instant Serge and the time she had spent with him was forgotten!

CHAPTER FIVE

Prince Charles de Courel was lavishly dressed from top to toe in a red jacket and epaulettes. A black cape was thrown aside over one shoulder and he had removed his white gloves and tucked them under his arm.

Diamond rings winked on his fingers and even the buttons of his cuffs seemed to flash showing that they too were of precious stones.

His hair was gold and his eyes were grey.

'Grey as goose-down,' thought Elvira dreamily.

He was her every idea of a real Prince and for the first time in her life she longed to possess what was not in her power to possess. How she would love to be courted by just such a lofty personage.

'*If he would only look my way once*,' she prayed fervently, quite forgetting her sombre dress and appearance.

Indeed so lost was she that she did not realise her hands were at her cheeks and her eyes shining.

Lord Baseheart stepped forward with a bow and welcomed the Prince to Baseheart Castle. The Prince inclined his head regally. Lady Cruddock then sank to a curtsy and the Prince graciously extended his hand to raise her up.

"*Madame*," he intoned and his deep French tones seemed to send a thrill round the assembled company.

Now Lord Baseheart ushered forward his daughter. Elvira watched enviously as the Prince took Delphine's hand and kissed it with effortless gallantry.

Delphine seemed to have lost all her bravado. She flushed deeply and was clearly nervous.

The Prince did not release her hand, but gazed deeply into her eyes. Though it sent a pang through Elvira's heart, she was at the same time greatly relieved.

Serge had said nothing!

Her gratitude that Serge had not betrayed her confidences was followed a second later by indignation that he had allowed her to divulge them in the first place.

Surely once he knew where she was bound he should have revealed the identity of his Master! She would not then have been so indiscreet.

She glanced round to see where the valet was. To her consternation she immediately caught his eye, for he had been watching her as intently as she had been watching the Prince. Her brows creased with displeasure.

"Elvira?" came Delphine's voice loudly. "Where are you, Elvira?"

Elvira looked quickly round.

"Elvira," Delphine called again. "Come. You must be presented to the Prince."

Forgetting Serge once again, Elvira shrank back behind the tall footman.

A moment ago she had longed for the Prince to look her way and now that she had been summoned, she was suddenly acutely aware of her plainness. Why had she not worn the tortoiseshell clasp instead of the dull yellow ribbon.

"*Elvira*!"

Delphine was insistent.

Slowly Elvira emerged from behind the footman and, head bent, legs seeming hardly able to bear her weight, she crossed the hallway to curtsy before the Prince.

Only at the last moment did she raise her eyes.

"This is my cousin and esteemed companion," Delphine was saying breathlessly. "We are most awfully good friends."

The Prince gave Elvira a glance and a cursory nod. Then his eyes were once more riveted on Delphine.

Elvira stood as if struck. She had not expected effusion on the part of the Prince, but to barely register with His Highness! She felt like an insect casually brushed from someone's shoulder.

She did not know whether she should retreat backwards or remain until dismissed. The only virtue in her present predicament was that it afforded her the opportunity to gaze on the object of her desire at close quarters.

He was so tall, so upright, so *Royal.* A curl of hair over his ear was the colour of corn. His eyelids were heavy and veined with blue. His expression as he gazed on Delphine was so – so ardent.

'Oh, if he would only look at me that way for one second, it would be the happiest second of my life!' thought Elvira.

"Elvira – you may go."

Lady Cruddock, who had been watching Elvira narrowly now waved her away.

Elvira turned and stumbled back the way she had come. She had never known herself to be in such a daze.

Someone stepped into her path as if to address her.

It was Serge.

She stared up at him and moved on without a word, leaving him gazing after her with a frown.

She found a chair at the back of the hall and sank gratefully down.

There were a few more formal greetings before the Prince and his valet were conducted to his suite. The assembled company began to disperse, some casting glances of curiosity towards Elvira where she sat brooding.

Elvira was soon left alone. It was only when she heard the chimes of midday that she roused herself and made her way to her room, only to be intercepted by Cassie.

"I've been looking all over for you, Miss Elvira. Miss Delphine wants you to attend her in her boudoir."

Delphine wants you.

It was like a dash of cold water in Elvira's face. What had she been doing, allowing herself to dwell on the Prince in this way? He was *Delphine*'s suitor – practically fiancé.

Without a word she followed Cassie to Delphine's room.

Delphine bounded towards her, bracelets madly jangling. Elvira's hands almost flew to her ears to block out the sound.

"Elvira, did you see the way he simply ate me up with his eyes? He's in love with me already. I know it! His lips lingered far longer on my hand than was necessary. When he said my name in such low tones – '*Mademoiselle Delfeeeeen*'– it made my heart flutter so! And he's brought me gifts. And this beautiful ruby brooch. And French perfume. Isn't it all just wonderful."

"Wonderful," echoed Elvira dutifully, though her heart felt as lead. "Wonderful," she said again and went over to the window, where she blinked back her tears against the dull sheen of the midday sun.

She wanted the Prince so much. The Prince who was destined for her cousin. She wanted his lips on *her* hand, his low voice in *her* ear.

Aunt Willis had accused her of envy in her letter and she had indignantly refuted the idea. But now – here it was. She felt sick with it, sick with envy of Delphine.

She was utterly downcast that her cousin had cast such an instant spell over the Prince while she, Elvira, had merited only a glance and a slight nod.

'What else could I have expected, dressed as I was like an impoverished governess,' she rebuked herself bitterly.

"I can't wait for supper," Delphine rattled on. "Aunt Cruddock has promised I shall be seated next to the Prince. I wish you could be there to see what passes between us. I'm sure at this rate I shall soon be as madly in love as he."

Elvira tapped a finger with seeming idleness on the glass.

"Didn't Aunt Cruddock advise you *not* to fall in love?" she reminded her cousin.

Delphine's face fell.

"She did and she said it was the only way to keep a man in your power. But – but I *want* to be in love with the

Prince. In fact, I think I already am. Oh, dear."

Elvira came away from the window.

"Would you object, cousin, if I go to my room now? I have a letter to write."

"What? Oh. Oh, yes. Of course. But just before you go, take these stockings with you. They need sewing at the heel and you've such delicate fingers."

Numbly Elvira took the stockings and departed.

In her room she sat by the fire and examined the stockings, which were silk, of course. She laid one of the stockings against her cheek and rocked gently to and fro. It was so soft.

She imagined the Prince kneeling to kiss Delphine's foot and his lips encountering this soft fabric just above her Chinese slipper –

With a sigh she fetched her sewing basket and set to work.

She was thus preoccupied when Lady Cruddock entered.

Elvira was so surprised to find that august figure in her room that she sprang up, upsetting her basket. Spools of thread went spinning across the floor and she knelt to retrieve them, but Lady Cruddock motioned her up irritably.

"Leave it for the moment. I haven't made my way up here to address your recumbent form."

Elvira rose from the floor.

"No, Lady Cruddock."

She waited as she perused the room, looked at Elvira's book with a scowl of disapproval and folded her arms.

"You took a great deal of interest in the Prince this morning."

"I-I did? Well – it is not often one encounters a Royal personage."

Lady Cruddock regarded her from under lowered lids.

"Come now. Nothing ever escapes my notice. *You wanted to be in my niece's shoes.* I saw it quite clearly if no one else did."

"I assure you," said Elvira after a pause, " that I am fully reconciled to wearing only the shoes that you and Lord Baseheart provide."

Lady Cruddock's eyelids fluttered.

"A very clever answer. Too clever, I fear. Delphine is rather a noodle beside you, but she's a *wealthy* noodle, so what does it matter?" She toyed a moment with her lorgnette. "Our coach driver, the one who conveyed you from the *White Doe Inn*, has told me a rather surprising story. Do you want to hear it?"

Fearing the worst, Elvira gave a barely perceptible nod.

"He told me," continued Lady Cruddock, "that the stranger who you passed a night with in a peasant's cottage has turned out to be none other than the Prince's valet. No doubt you were rather taken aback yourself when you saw him?"

Elvira let out her breath.

"Yes, Lady Cruddock. I was."

"You had no prior knowledge of his position?"

"None."

"I suppose I have no choice but to believe you. Strange, though, that you did not also encounter the Prince that night."

Elvira said nothing and Lady Cruddock walked to the door and paused.

"Delphine the noodle has prevailed upon her father to allow you to join us at supper. Against his better judgement and mine, I might add."

She sailed out of the room.

Elvira sat down again and picked up her sewing, but she was unable to work.

She was torn between excitement at the thought of sitting at supper with the Prince and reluctance to witness his inevitable attentions to Delphine.

*

It was the custom for Delphine and Elvira to take tea together at three o'clock each afternoon. Today the tea table was set up before a roaring fire in Delphine's room. Elvira was surprised to discover Lady Cruddock present as well.

She was further surprised when Lord Baseheart joined them, although he did not sit at table, but paced the room as if agitated.

"Odd request from the Prince via his valet," he blurted out at last. "Seems His Highness wants the valet to dine with us tonight."

"It's probably the custom in France to appease one's inferiors," snorted Lady Cruddock. "After all they might still cut off your head as soon as look at you!"

Lord Baseheart glanced irritably at his sister.

"Quite. Though this is not so much a case of custom as of practicality. It appears the Prince speaks barely a word of English, while his valet is fluent."

"A nation has come to a pretty pass when valets are better educated than their Masters!" sniffed Lady Cruddock.

"It seems the valet was brought up in England." Lord Baseheart made an impatient gesture. "And, contrary to our previous understanding, the valet informs us that the Prince was brought up by his mother in France."

Lady Cruddock set her lips.

"Whatever the case, we must nip this notion of His Highness in the bud. We cannot have servants sitting with us at table."

"I daresay." Lord Baseheart looked uncomfortable.

"The Prince is your guest and should observe the social proprieties of England whilst he is here," went on Lady Cruddock firmly. "He must fend for himself at supper and after all Delphine has been taking French lessons. As long as she is able to converse with her fiancé, what do the rest of us matter?"

"I haven't been studying that hard, aunt!" Delphine looked alarmed.

"I don't think the Prince will mind how hard you have been studying," smiled Lord Baseheart.

"No," simpered Delphine, a dreamy look entering her eye. "He's smitten already, isn't he, Papa? And I do rather like him. He is *so* handsome!"

Lord Baseheart rubbed his hands together.

"I wouldn't care if he looked like a water butt! He brings a highly desirable title into the family!"

Elvira, who had been listening quietly all this while, bit her lip. It was terrible to hear the Prince discussed in such an irreverent tone.

The conversation had enlightened her on one point, however. She had been correct as to why it was the valet who remained with her during the snowstorm and not his Master.

She and the Prince would have been unable to exchange a single word!

*

"Seems this snow is never going to melt!" grumbled Beth, as she laid out a fresh petticoat for Elvira. "Over a month now it's lain there and more falls every day."

"I am used to it," admitted Elvira. "It makes everything seem – dreamlike."

Beth, smoothing out the petticoat, threw her a glance.

"I've no time for dreamlike. I like to know what's real and what's not. And what's real is that I'm going to have to go and live in France or find a new place."

"Live in France, Beth?" Elvira gave a start. "Why should you have to do that?"

"You haven't been putting your mind to what's about to happen, have you, miss? Miss Delphine's like as not going to marry this Prince, right? And he's going to take her back to France to live. Right?"

"I – suppose so, Beth."

"Suppose so? Bless me, you couldn't have thought they'd live here at Baseheart? No. Miss Delphine will go to France and she'll want her companion – that's you – to accompany her. And I should hope her companion would want her maid to accompany her."

Elvira had raised her head and was staring at the frosted window. She had simply never considered the matter, but it was true – she *would* go to France. Neither

Lord Baseheart nor his sister would have any use for her at Baseheart after the departure of Delphine.

Beth regarded her curiously.

"Don't you want to go to France, miss? I do. I've heard it's beautiful and the people sing a lot and dance on grapes to make wine. I'd like to do that. Miss?"

Elvira looked round slowly.

"I daresay I should like to go to France, Beth."

She was thinking of the globe in the study at Aunt Willis's and the hours she had spent tracing a finger over its surface, exploring the world in her imagination.

Yes, she would like to visit France. But to live there as companion? To see every day the burgeoning happiness of her cousin and the Prince? To be so close to the man she loved and to never be important to him in any way? What torture that would be!

"Come on, miss," urged Beth. "You must hurry. Supper is sharp at six."

"Which dress shall I wear, Beth?" she asked with a rueful twist to her lips. "Which is the – the least ugly?"

"I'm afraid, miss, it's not in our hands to decide," said Beth looking unhappy. "Lady Cruddock told me that she's sending up a new garment. I'm surprised it hasn't arrived yet."

"Perhaps," put in Elvira hopefully, "perhaps she has decided that I should have something a little more fashionable, since it is a supper in honour of the Prince."

"Perhaps – " muttered Beth, but she looked very doubtful.

Her doubts were confirmed a minute later when a housemaid tapped at the door.

"Lady Cruddock sent this up," said the maid with a

bob and a barely suppressed grin.

Beth and Elvira regarded the latest addition to her miserable wardrobe. It was grey of a coarse cloth with a high stiff neck.

"I might as well wear sackcloth and ashes," commented Elvira with more bitterness than Beth had yet heard in her voice.

"It's a shame, that's what it is!" muttered Beth. "But never you mind, miss, even in sackcloth you're much more beautiful than Miss Delphine."

"Am I really, Beth?"

"Everyone thinks so," added Beth indiscreetly.

"Except – except the Prince."

"The Prince?" Beth regarded her Mistress sharply.

"He's *so* very handsome, isn't he?" sighed Elvira.

"He's good looking enough," shrugged Beth, "but that valet of his, Serge, he's the handsomer by far."

"*Serge*?" Elvira was astonished.

"Yes, miss," said Beth. "All the kitchen maids are quite soft on him! Put a red coat on his back and rings on his fingers and he'd look more of a Prince than the Prince!"

"What silly nonsense!" retorted Elvira, mortally offended. "He's handsome enough for a valet, but that's as far as it goes."

She had quite forgotten how enraptured she had felt clasped against Serge's breast that night at the cottage and how she had relaxed in his strong and tender arms before mounting the ladder to the loft under the stars.

The Prince had vanquished the potency of such memories from her mind and the only sentiment she nursed towards Serge was displeasure.

Beth said nothing more. She helped Elvira into the grey dress and stood back while she regarded herself in the mirror.

If she ignored the dress and looked only at her face, she might feel a little more confident. After all, her eyes were large and lustrous and wide apart and as blue as an azure sea. Her hair had a burnished sheen and fell to her waist like a mantle. Her skin was the colour of the snow, but translucent with just a faint flush.

Surely, *surely* the Prince must notice her tonight?

She leaned close and pinched her cheeks until they glowed with colour. Then she took a blue ribbon and tied up her hair, revealing her long graceful neck.

Beth looked after her as she departed. Something had changed in her Mistress, but she had as yet no idea what it was!

Elvira, her head full of fancy, descended the first narrow stairway as if the Prince was waiting for her. She held her head so high and proud that the grey coarse dress was almost an irrelevance.

On the first landing a figure stepped quietly out of the shadows.

"Elvira!"

She gave a start, her hand to her breast.

"S-Serge."

He regarded her wryly.

"Ah, I have just been wondering whether you remembered me at all. You barely looked my way when my – Master and I arrived."

Elvira regarded him coldly.

"And I have just been wondering why you did not see fit to inform me of the identity of your Master when we were marooned in that cottage. You deceived me, sir!"

"Deceived you?" Serge stood very still.

His look was so stern, his eyes so dark, that Elvira looked away.

"You knew I was en route for Baseheart," she complained, but with a less confident vehemence. "Why did you not tell me that you and your Master were bound for the same destination?"

Serge was silent for a moment and then gave a sigh.

"Think of it as the natural reticence attendant on anyone connected to – the world of Royalty. We must learn to hold our tongues."

"You did not instruct me to hold mine!" parried Elvira.

The shadow of a smile hovered on Serge's lips.

"No. I was too enchanted by your voice."

"What could possibly enchant you about my voice?"

Serge leaned an elbow on the banister and regarded her with amusement.

"Good heavens, madam, do you have so little knowledge of your charms? Not only did you once inform me that you had no beauty, you are now professing astonishment that your voice should give pleasure."

"It d-does? Why?" Elvira felt herself reddening.

Serge half closed his eyes as he answered,

"Because it is as musical as the song of a lark and as sweet as the rush of a sparkling stream. It would please any man."

With an unthinking innocence, Elvira caught her

breath.

"Would it please – a Prince?"

Serge was silent a moment and when he spoke it was with a certain sad gravity.

"Yes, indeed, madam. It would please a Prince."

Elvira felt instant alarm that he had guessed her secret and she tried to lighten her tone for her next remark.

"Well, I am relieved that I can at least please our guest's ear tonight, for I shall certainly not please his eye!"

Serge now looked her up and down, taking in her unattractive dress and guessing that it was no choice of her own, he softened.

"Believe me, you will please his eye, too, madam."

Elvira blushed again. Her eye strayed restlessly to the stairway, which she must descend to reach the dining room and the Prince. Serge stepped aside with a bow.

"But I must detain you no longer."

Elvira put her foot onto the first step and then turned,

"I am sorry that you will not be at supper," she said with great sincerity.

Serge smiled down at her.

"Oh, but I shall be. Not at table, I admit, but I am to serve the Prince and act as his interpreter. Your uncle agreed to it."

Before Elvira could make any comment the gong sounded in the hall below.

"I must hurry!" she cried and set off as Serge watched her slender form trip lightly down the stairs.

Elvira was placed at the extreme end of the table. She had a gouty old Count on one side and a grizzled old

Peer on the other, neither of whom seemed inclined to address a single word to her.

She didn't care. She barely registered the presence of Serge, who stood dutifully behind his Master's chair and helped serve him from the dishes that arrived one after the other.

She only had eyes for the Prince. She watched enviously as he and Delphine fully engaged with each other.

Indeed it began to seem as if there was nobody else in the room. Their eyes were locked on one another, their hands touching at regular intervals.

Soon the Prince was holding wine-drenched bread to Delphine's lips, while she in her turn took a morsel of plump goose flesh on her fork and held it out to the Prince.

Lady Cruddock almost dropped her lorgnettes at this sight, while Lord Baseheart looked most disgruntled.

The gouty old Count next to Elvira gave a grunt.

"Funny sort of behaviour for a Prince."

"Indeed," agreed the grizzled Peer. "And did you notice how he used the wrong spoon for the soup?"

"Probably doesn't even *own* a spoon himself," cackled the Count. "He's only marrying Miss Baseheart for the family silver."

Elvira was scandalised.

"You are speaking most disrespectfully of your host's future son-in-law!" she stated stiffly.

The Peer and the Count looked across her at each other, but seemed to feel it beneath their dignity to reply. They moved on to other topics, leaving Elvira free to her own interpretation of the Prince's behaviour.

'It is part of his Gallic charm,' she decided, 'to be so

natural and informal.'

Nevertheless, when the Prince plucked a rose from a flower bowl to present to Delphine, she saw Serge lean down and speak in his Master's ear. The Prince listened and shrugged, but straightened up in his chair.

Serge seems to have some hold over him, Elvira thought in amazement.

After dessert, Lord Baseheart rose to propose a toast welcoming the Prince to Baseheart. Glasses clinked.

The Prince glanced at Serge and stood to make a response.

"*Mesdames et messieurs, je vous remercie tous*," he said with a most dazzling smile and, head tipped back, dispatched a full glass of champagne.

Elvira gazed on in rapture. How wonderful his voice sounded, so deep and romantic.

How his gold hair glinted in the light of a hundred candles. How his eyes gleamed and there was a daredevil cast to his expression. If he was not a Prince he might have been a – a pirate on the high seas.

If only, for one moment of that entire evening, he had cast his eye her way!

CHAPTER SIX

It was an icy afternoon and Delphine, wrapped in furs, was strolling in the garden with the Prince. She clung on his arm and giggled at his every remark, although it was doubtful if she understood a single word.

Following them Elvira eyed the train of Delphine's cloak trailing in the snow. How she would have liked to tread on it – oh, so lightly – and see it slide from her shoulders!

Anything to interrupt the extravagant display of courtship that went on daily under everyone's nose.

Since protocol demanded that Delphine and her suitor should never be left alone together, Elvira had been forced to spend many hours in their wake.

Serge usually joined them to aid the Prince in his halting attempts at conversation with Delphine.

As the days passed, however, eyes and hands began to do the work of translation. Serge became redundant and yet still he accompanied his Master.

Elvira would glance at the valet and find his eyes fixed so broodingly on the couple ahead that at last a wondrous thought struck her.

'*Serge has fallen in love with Delphine just as she has fallen in love with the Prince!*'

She heard the crunch of Serge's boots on the snow behind her and imagined him feeling as desolate as herself at the constant display of the lovebirds.

Then she almost blushed as if he could read her thoughts. She was sure he would not relish knowing that she had guessed his secret nor would he welcome her sympathy.

Ahead of her Delphine and the Prince stopped in front of the frozen lake.

The Prince drew even closer to her and murmured something in her ear. Delphine let out a peel of laughter that sounded to Elvira like the cracking of thin ice.

She shivered and drew her cape tight about her shoulders glad of its thick folds.

That it was the cape Serge had given her at the old woman's cottage did not escape her awareness.

She had offered to return it to Serge the very day after his arrival, but he had seemed to guess that it was her only protection against the bitter cold.

Since that polite exchange, neither she nor Serge had alluded to the night they had passed together at the cottage.

It was as if it had never occurred.

She started as she heard Serge's soft voice at her elbow.

"The air is more than usually icy this afternoon."

She stared down, stirring the soft snow with the toe of her boot.

Before Serge could say any more, Delphine turned at the lake and called to him.

"Find us some stones to skim over the lake, will you?"

Elvira flinched at her cousin's imperious tone, but Serge did not hesitate. Taking his cap from his head, he knelt to scour the ground.

Delphine's eyes met Elvira's for a moment and flashed with something like amusement before turning to link her arm again with the Prince.

Elvira had already seen this look in her cousin's eye. Delphine treated the valet with little courtesy and was often downright rude to him, knowing that the Prince could not understand what she was saying and seemed oblivious to her tone.

She confessed to Elvira that it was a game she enjoyed, particularly as the more unpleasant she was to Serge, the more attentive he proved to her requests.

Delphine sensed that the valet would never dare complain about his treatment to his Master.

"The Prince is just too besotted with me," she would sigh contentedly.

Elvira looked down at Serge searching for loose stones and on an impulse, she knelt beside him. He regarded her with surprise.

"I'll help you," she offered, removing her gloves with her teeth.

Moving snow aside with her bare hands, she quickly uncovered four stones, which she held out in triumph. Serge had found four as well and he took Elvira's with a nod. Delphine grabbed them without a by-your-leave and she and the Prince began to skim them over the frozen lake.

Elvira's hands were feeling numb and she blew on her fingers to warm them. Serge regarded her sternly.

"You have no fur muff?"

"No," she shrugged.

Abruptly Serge seized her hand and began to chaff it between his own. Elvira was too taken aback to react.

Her hands seemed lost in Serge's clasp, his palms were warm and gradually her fingers began to tingle with returning blood. He raised his eyes and she blinked.

For a second his expression was almost ardent. Then that look was gone to be replaced by his usual remote gaze. She withdrew her hands.

"T-thank you."

Serge gave a curt nod, turned towards the lake and a scowl crossed his brow.

The Prince and Delphine had used up their stones and she had picked up a fallen bough and was leaning out over the lake, attempting to break a section of ice with the Prince holding her by the waist.

Elvira, sharing Serge's displeasure, began to pull on her gloves.

"They are so – happy together," she sighed, disguising her unhappiness with a smile.

Serge's jaw clenched.

"You think so?"

"Yes. They are well suited."

Serge gave a harsh laugh.

"You could not be more wrong. The truth is, she is far too good for *him*."

Elvira could not contain her astonishment.

"But he is a Prince! How could she be too good for him? He is so – so handsome – his every gesture so regal."

Serge's pupils became as dark as the night sky and she almost shrank before their baleful expression.

"So regal, eh? Do you not mistake the apparel for the man?"

Elvira drew herself up with indignation.

"You think me so shallow, sir?"

"I think you – so inexperienced," replied Serge.

"You do not have to be experienced to know a Royal nature when you see it."

"You would never mistake me then for a Prince?"

"You? *Never*!"

Hardly had she spoken than Elvira felt ashamed. Serge was suffering as she was and just as she longed to be in Delphine's place, he longed to be in the Prince's. It was cruel of her to be so dismissive.

"Perhaps," she relented, "if you were wearing just such a cloak – with its fur collar – and just such diamonds."

"Perhaps – "

Another squeal of delight from Delphine and he had lost interest in Elvira's thoughts. His eyes once more settled on the couple at the lakeside.

"Have you been in the Prince's employ long?" she ventured.

"He and I have known each other many years."

"Has he been – a good Master?"

Serge hesitated.

"Perhaps it is he who should answer that question and not me," he replied at last.

Elvira was perplexed by this answer, but had no time to brood over it.

Delphine had announced that she was ready for tea and the party made its way back to the castle, where the table was laid out in Delphine's sitting room.

Serge made his excuses and left, while Elvira took her cup and plate to the window seat. From there she had a view of the glittering white world outside.

It was her only distraction as Delphine and the Prince had not one word to say to her. She was describing the plans for the coming Christmas Ball and he nodded and smiled over his hot chocolate as if he followed every word.

Every loving look the Prince cast Delphine's way was a knife in Elvira's heart.

*

The day of the ball dawned and Elvira was summoned to Delphine's room. Seated at her dressing table she looked up as Elvira entered.

"The Prince is going to propose to me tonight, I am certain," she said breathlessly. "Have you ever seen a man more in love than he, Elvira?"

"No," agreed Elvira. She could not help but stare at her cousin in the dressing table mirror.

Delphine looked almost pretty, her skin glowed and her eyes were shining.

Without thinking, Elvira took up a hairbrush and ran its bristles across her fingers.

"Don't just stand there playing!" scolded Delphine. "Brush my hair for me!"

Elvira obeyed.

"The Prince will propose while we're dancing," mused Delphine. "I'm sure of it. I'll be in his arms and my heart will be pounding and he will say '*will you do me the honour of becoming my wife*?' And I'll say, '*yes, my darling, yes*!' Then Papa will announce the betrothal before all the guests and – ouch! That hurt."

"I'm s-sorry!" mumbled Elvira.

Delphine, too absorbed in her fantasy to be other than quickly mollified, began toying with her perfume bottles.

"It's a pity you won't be there to see it all. I think it's truly horrid of Aunt Cruddock and Papa. What harm would it do?"

"None, I'm sure," replied Elvira. "But I daresay I should look out of place without a gown."

A spasm of sympathy crossed Delphine's face and she sprang up from the stool.

"Look – here in my wardrobe, I have so many gowns, please take one!"

"I-I couldn't!"

"Of course you could. Why not? Take this one."

Elvira stared at the coral pink dress that Delphine held up before her.

"It's – beautiful," she sighed faintly. "But I am sure your aunt will not agree to let me come to the ball."

"Maybe not, but have it anyway." She thrust the gown into Elvira's arms. "You may have occasion to wear it one day and then you can think of me. I'm really quite generous, aren't I?"

Elvira nodded, stupefied, as she caught the gown against her breast.

"You better take it away now," warned Delphine. "Cassie will be here any minute to dress me."

Elvira hurried back to her room. She spread the coral pink dress on her bed and sat, chin in hand, gazing at it.

The guests began to arrive at seven o'clock and Elvira could hear the carriages roll up to the front door.

Then she heard the orchestra strike up, far away, as if in some distant and subterranean cavern.

She went to the window and stared out. The glitter of candlelight was thrown onto the lawn from the ballroom windows.

She turned and looked at the dress again.

What harm would it do to put on the dress and *pretend* she was going to the ball!

She took off the brown dress she was wearing and quickly slipped on the coral dress. Holding the back together with one hand, she gazed at herself in the pier glass.

She did not dare call for Beth to hook her up, so she cast around for a pin.

Finding one she finally succeeded in securing the dress half way up her back. It would not do, but she was not going to be seen anyway!

Fixing Beth's tortoiseshell clasp on the side of her head, she stepped before the pier glass.

If only the Prince could see her now!

The ballroom below must have become stuffy for someone threw open the French windows and the strains of the violins spilled out into the night. The sound lured Elvira as if by a magnet to be nearer the music, to catch a forbidden glimpse of the ladies in their ball-gowns!

Silent as a shadow, she left her room. She almost glided along the corridor and down the stairs. It was pure chance that she met no one.

She crossed the Great Hall and along a corridor that led to the kitchen garden. Opening the last door, she walked outside.

The air was sharp as a blade but she barely felt it. Holding the hem of her dress high, she made her way round to the terrace outside the ballroom.

Apart from where light flowed out from the long windows, the terrace was in darkness and Elvira was invisible to the dancers she saw moving in silhouette in the ballroom.

She stood listening as a faint breeze fluttered the net of her gown.

'This is *my* very own ballroom,' she decided and began to dance.

She imagined she was in *his* arms, the Prince's arms. She imagined his breath on her cheek, his arm about her waist.

Eyes closed she danced like a silver moonbeam across the terrace.

The waltz ended and in the lull, Elvira stretched forth her arms with longing, imagining they might enfold the Prince. Eyes still closed, she could almost sense him in front of her.

Someone grasped her hands and drew her close. Her heart hammered violently within her breast.

It was he, it was her beloved!

She dared not look – she hardly dared breathe.

Then an all too familiar voice murmured in her ear.

"May I have the next dance?"

With a gasp her eyes flew open.

It was the valet, Serge!

She struggled in his arms.

"Let – me – go!" she whispered fiercely.

“Let you go?” His voice was hoarse. “When the music will soon begin again?”

His grip was irresistible. She felt the force of his will as his arm slid about her waist.

‘I am held together with a pin,’ she remembered in sudden panic and flinched as Serge’s hand discovered the unfastened back of her gown.

He leaned his head back to stare down at her.

“What’s this?”

“I-I had no one to hook my dress.”

His hand still lingered on her back and she felt her bare flesh ripple under the pressure of his warm fingers.

With a shock, she realised that his touch aroused a degree of pleasure within her. What emotion Serge felt she could not tell, but she sensed a tremor run through his frame before he stepped away and turned her about.

“I will do up your gown,” he proposed, his tone gentler than before.

She stood trembling while Serge carefully began to slip each hook into its corresponding eye. Now and then she threw a fearful glance at the ballroom. Supposing someone should come out? But, though one or two windows were open, no one emerged.

She seemed to be on fire. Her cheeks flamed, her bare shoulders felt flushed, but how could this be, when it was not the Prince who stood behind her but Serge, his valet?

“It’s done,” murmured Serge.

She thought he might move away, but he did not. She felt his hand move to her neck, where he ran his fingers up into her luxuriant mass of hair.

She froze as she sensed him bring the tresses to his

lips.

The moon came riding out from behind a bank of inky cloud and its seemingly foolish face winked down at her. Stars sailed alongside, twinkling like – like the diamonds on the Prince's fingers!

Yes, she must think of the Prince. *He* was the one she loved, even if her love was illicit. She must resist this potent spell that Serge sought to cast upon her. She had seen the effect of his personality on that serving wench at the *White Doe Inn*.

He was a seducer. Well, she, Elvira Carrisford, was not going to fall into his net!

"Thank you for your help, sir," she said stiffly.

In response, Serge placed his hands on her shoulders and turned her round to face him. In the pale moonlight, his eyes seemed lit from within, their pupils large and black as a forest pool.

She felt she was drowning in his intense gaze, while behind him, the orchestra struck up another waltz.

"Dance with me," he muttered softly and drew her again into his arms.

She could no longer resist.

She was light as gossamer, she was a note in the melody that streamed forth from the open windows. Treetops fluttered against the night sky, stars seemed to hover like silver moths.

She yielded her whole being to the dance. Eyes closed, she was no longer sure who was leading her across the stone flagging of the terrace.

Was it Serge or the Prince? They were becoming inextricably linked in her imagination. She did not know whose arms she would rather have around her.

Then Serge leaned down, his lips brushing her temple as he spoke.

"Elvira – tell me – who are you dreaming about?"

At that moment, so confused was she, it might well have been Serge's name that she uttered.

But it was not.

"The Prince," she mumbled.

She felt Serge stiffen and the hand that held hers relaxed its grip.

Her eyes fluttered open as he stepped away.

"The waltz has ended," he said, turning towards the ballroom.

She hung her head unhappily. Of course! She had overstepped the bounds of propriety by declaring an interest in his Master when he was as good as engaged to Delphine.

Another door was flung open to allow air into the ballroom. Within the voice of a footman declared loudly that an announcement was about to be made.

To Elvira's surprise, Serge uttered a quiet oath under his breath and moved towards the nearest window.

Elvira hesitated a moment and then followed to stand beside him. He did not so much as glance her way. His eyes were fixed rigidly on the figure of Lord Baseheart as he climbed the steps of the orchestra dais.

Seeing Delphine and the Prince make their way to stand beside him, Elvira's heart began to thud.

Delphine's face was aglow, her hands clasped together with excitement.

The Prince's eyes were searching the crowd. They swept towards the window and settled on Serge's face and for a moment, the two men, Master and valet, regarded each other in silence while the assembled guests jostled forward.

Then, to Elvira's astonishment, the Prince gave a slight and almost guilty shrug of his shoulders, as if to say that what was about to happen was out of his control.

Serge lifted a hand and leaned it against the window. His other hand, Elvira noticed, clenched itself into a fist at his side.

Lord Baseheart cleared his throat.

"Ladies and gentlemen and dear friends. I wish to announce that I have just given my blessing to the betrothal of my beloved daughter, Delphine Juliet Baseheart to Prince Charles de Courel. The nuptials will take place in four months time."

Despite herself, Elvira let out a soft cry of anguish.

Serge wheeled round to stare at her and then, eyes ablaze, he strode off into the darkness of the night.

Unthinking, Elvira turned and stumbled two or three paces after him before stopping. Hand to her breast, she stood in heartfelt misery as his figure crossed the lawn and disappeared into the row of trees.

'He is so in love with Delphine,' thought Elvira. 'But how can I console him, who am so in love with his Master? What words of comfort can I give, who is as desolate as he?'

She wondered at the Prince's guilty shrug just before the announcement. What had it signified? Perhaps the Prince knew that his valet was in love with Delphine.

How kind of him and how very considerate to acknowledge in advance the despair that the news was bound to arouse in Serge's breast!

Elvira could hear the cries of congratulations that had greeted Lord Baseheart's speech. She stood for a moment staring at the figures on the other side of the window and then with a sigh she retraced her steps to her room.

She found Beth in the act of turning down the bed.

"Bless me, miss!" the maid cried in amazement. "What a picture you look. I never knew you had such a dress with you! Surely you didn't go to the ball after all?"

Elvira did not reply but moved wearily to the pier glass.

"Unhook me, please, will you?"

"Who hooked you up in the first place, is what I'd like to know," grumbled Beth, but a look from Elvira silenced her. She helped her out of the dress and stood with it draped over her arm as Elvira climbed into bed.

"Have you heard the news, miss?" she asked warily.

"About the betrothal? Yes, Beth, I have. I – would rather not discuss it at present, though. I am feeling rather tired."

She buried her face in the pillow in such a way as to indicate a dismissal. Beth hung the dress in the wardrobe and tiptoed out.

The pillow was wet with tears before the door closed behind her.

*

Elvira heard the clock strike midnight and the sound of guests departing.

She turned over and stared at the moonlit room.

The noises of the house settling down for the night continued until the clock struck one, but she was still wide awake.

After tossing and turning for another hour Elvira suddenly realised she was hungry. She had not eaten all evening and perhaps that was why she could not sleep.

It would be quite unfair at this hour to ring for poor Beth, so there was only one thing to do and that was to go down to the kitchen herself.

She climbed out of bed and put on her slippers. She groped for her candle, took it to the still glimmering coals in the grate and lit the wick.

The house was quiet as a tomb and Elvira crept by the kitchen maids asleep on their cots in the scullery. In the pantry she found bread and cheese and a piece of game pie. With these in her hand she made her way back into the corridor.

Glancing towards the door that led to the kitchen garden, she saw that it was ajar.

Who could have been so careless as not to bolt it for the night?

A second later she froze as she heard low voices in the garden beyond.

Who was up at this hour besides herself?

The voices moved out of earshot so Elvira tiptoed forward and peered out.

Pacing the paths of the kitchen garden were two figures.

She suppressed a gasp as she recognised Serge and the Prince.

Whatever subject they were discussing, they were in obvious disagreement. Though their voices were low, they were heated.

Serge seemed particularly incensed, turning round

on the gravel and raising his fist in the air. The Prince hissed replies, looked away and kicked at one of the posts supporting a washing line.

Then, to Elvira's absolute shock, Serge caught hold of the Prince by his collar.

Her hands flew to her mouth.

The scene before her was incomprehensible. How could a servant address his Master in such a manner? How could a Prince allow it? Surely Serge would be sent on his way tomorrow without a penny and no references?

The Prince extricated himself from Serge's grip. He stood for a moment glaring at his servant. He then gave what looked like a reluctant nod and, turning on his heels, stormed off towards the garden gate.

Elvira shrank back, grateful that he was not coming her way. Peeping out after a moment, she saw Serge standing with head bowed as if lost in thought.

Elvira slipped away and back in her room she spread out her meal, but she could not eat.

All that was on her mind was the scene in the garden. What could have been the disagreement? Was it the betrothal announced that very evening?

Whatever the cause of the quarrel, Elvira realised one thing with a certain degree of surprise.

She would be most upset if Serge was dismissed from the Prince's service!

CHAPTER SEVEN

The sound of barking dogs rang out in the frosty morning air. Elvira threw aside her bedclothes and ran to the window.

Far below stood two grooms each holding two horses by the bridle. Three spaniels sported about a gamekeeper, excited beyond measure at the sight of the shotguns slung on his shoulder.

Lord Baseheart and the Prince emerged from the house, followed by an elderly Duke who had stayed on at Baseheart after last night's ball.

There was no sign of Serge.

The Prince cut a distinguished figure, but was evidently ill at ease. He paced to and fro, tugging at his gloves as if unaccustomed to such thick leather.

Lord Baseheart, the Duke and the gamekeeper mounted their steeds without aid. One of the grooms then knelt and, hands cupped, helped the Prince on to his horse and the party set off.

"Come away from there, miss, before you freeze," came Beth's voice behind Elvira.

She closed the window and sat down before the breakfast that Beth had brought her.

"Have you seen Serge about this morning?" she

asked her maid carefully.

"Serge? Can't say as I have, miss. I'd thought he'd gone out on the shoot."

Elvira considered. If Serge *had* been dismissed, then it was not as yet common knowledge.

Why should she care if Serge stayed at Baseheart? He was nothing to her! And yet – she and he shared a history.

He had rescued her from peril, cared for her when she was fevered and danced with her when she had no partner but her dreams. Like her, he nursed a secret love for someone out of his reach.

If he was gone, she would feel quite alone in her misery.

After breakfast, she dressed and went to Delphine's room, where she found her cousin still in her peignoir and looking petulant.

"The Prince did not send me greetings before he set out this morning," she complained. "He could have sent a note or a rose – anything. Indeed, now we are formally engaged, he could have come to my room to bid me adieu."

"That would not have been correct and it is as well that he knew it," remarked Elvira quietly.

Delphine threw her a sly look.

"Oh, he's not one for such outmoded concerns! He's always trying to get me alone, you know."

"He should not do so," commented Elvira shocked. Surely the Prince would not be so importunate?

Delphine gave a great bay of laughter.

"What could you possibly know of such matters, cousin? You've never been courted in your life. Unless you were courted the night you were alone with the valet at that cottage?"

Elvira blushed so deeply that Delphine felt she had quite hit the mark.

"He kissed you, Elvira, admit it!" she squealed.

"He did not!" riposted Elvira stoutly.

"Don't believe you," said Delphine, but she had already lost interest in a subject that did not directly involve her. Desultorily she picked up a powder puff and began to apply it to her nose.

"My nose shines so in the morning," she sighed. "What am I going to do, when I wake up beside the Prince? I daresay I shall have to keep a puff beneath my pillow."

An image of Delphine and the Prince lying together in a lavish bed with gold curtains rose so vividly in Elvira's mind that she turned away to the window.

"Serge did not accompany the Prince on the shoot this morning," she said as casually as she could.

Delphine stared from amid a cloud of powder, the puff arrested mid-air.

"He didn't? That's strange."

"Isn't it!" agreed Elvira. She began to trace the letters of a name on the window. *Prince Charles de Courel* it would have read, if visible.

"What are you doing there?" asked Delphine irritably. "Come away. I need to send you on an errand. I've a great desire for some preserved figs."

"Figs?" repeated Elvira.

"Yes. You'll find some in the pantry, I shouldn't wonder."

Happy to escape the overpowering scent of powder, Elvira departed.

She found the figs and a little wicker basket. Then feeling a headache coming on, she decided to take a quick turn in the garden before returning to her cousin.

Basket on her arm, she circled the kitchen garden slowly, drawing in great gulps of fresh air.

Next she saw Serge piling logs into a wheelbarrow. He glanced up, wiped his forehead with his arm and returned to his task without acknowledging her.

It was as if all memory of their dance by moonlight had vanished from his mind.

Elvira drew near and stood, swinging the basket of figs to and fro. She could hardly say she was glad to see Serge still at Baseheart without revealing that she had overheard the heated exchange the night before.

"I was surprised – you did not ride out with the Prince," she ventured at last.

"Were you? Why?" grunted Serge.

"You are – always with him."

"Like a shadow?" Serge gave a wry laugh

"Not a shadow, exactly. More like – his other self."

Serge glanced at her sharply.

"How could a valet be the other self of a Prince?"

Elvira's confidence grew even less sure.

"Well – you are his voice. We understand him through you. Without you, he is an enigma."

Serge threw down a log heavily.

"You take a great interest in the Prince. Are you in love with the blackguard?"

Elvira recoiled in shock.

"B-blackguard? How can you refer to your Master in such a manner?"

Serge reached out and caught at her wrist.

"Answer me. Are you in love with him?"

"It's n-not your business!"

She tried hard to pull her wrist away, but his grip tightened. His eyes were angry, his breast heaving with some inner conflict as he placed his free hand about the nape of her neck and forced her head towards him.

The next moment his lips were pressed harshly, yet heatedly, to hers.

Her breast rose in a tumult and the basket fell from her grasp.

She struggled, relented, struggled again and only when she felt close to swooning did he release her. She stood, heart pounding, blood drumming in her ears.

She wanted to castigate him but could not.

Through a mist she saw him lift a shovel, strike its blade into the earth and lean on the handle.

"Go," he muttered. "Before I can no longer answer for myself."

Turning, Elvira stumbled back along the path. She slammed the kitchen door and leaned panting against it.

'What a nerve, to kiss *me*,' she thought, 'just because he could not kiss my cousin!'

He's a brute, a common oaf, she decided, while yet her hand rose wonderingly to touch her lips and relive his kisses.

*

The shooting party did not return until late afternoon and Elvira was descending the stairs on her way to the library to find a book, when she saw Lord Baseheart. He threw a cursory glance at her before striding over to the fire blazing in the large marble hearth.

"The fellow's surprisingly inept in the field," he muttered to the air.

Wondering who Lord Baseheart meant by 'fellow', Elvira hurried on.

That evening, Delphine and Elvira walked down together to supper. Elvira trembled as she entered the dining room, aware that Serge was already present. To her relief he did not even glance her way.

Delphine, however, was bitterly disappointed when the Prince barely acknowledged her entrance. After all, they had not seen each other since the night before.

Throughout supper, it became obvious that the Prince was doing everything in his power to avoid his valet's eye. He played with his cutlery and ran his finger over the pattern on the table cloth.

Elvira surmised that this chill between the two men was connected to the argument in the garden and they had clearly not spoken since.

Over dessert Lady Cruddock began to expound on her plans for the nuptials. She would take Delphine to Gloucester to purchase silk for the wedding dress, hire an orchestra for the wedding breakfast and order a four-tiered cake from a French baker. This was to please the Prince, but he seemed not to have heard.

Delphine regarded her fiancé miserably. Was he not interested in their forthcoming wedding?

At last Serge gave a gesture of impatience and leaned to speak to the Prince. An expression of alarm crossed the Prince's features before he gave a reluctant nod.

Serge looked at Lord Baseheart and cleared his throat.

"Your Lordship."

Lord Baseheart looked up and Serge continued.

"The Prince requests a private meeting with you. Tonight."

All eyes turned towards the Prince, who looked uncomfortable at being suddenly the focus of attention. Lord Baseheart, meanwhile, gave a slight bow to his future son-in-law.

"Alas, I have arranged to visit my lawyer at his house in Chidford this evening. Perhaps the Prince and I might converse tomorrow morning? If that is acceptable to His Highness."

Serge hesitated before conveying this message to his Master. The Prince, seeming relieved, inclined his head towards Lord Baseheart.

Elvira supposed his visit to his lawyer was to discuss the details of Delphine's dowry. If that was what the Prince also wished to discuss, it was indeed better to wait until tomorrow.

After supper, Delphine and Elvira were making their way gloomily upstairs when a maid ran after them with a note addressed to *Miss Baseheart*. Delphine waved the maid away and opened the note. Her eyes grew wide with relief and excitement as she read its contents.

"The Prince has asked me to meet him in the garden – *alone*!"

"That is an improper request, cousin," commented Elvira.

Delphine pressed her hands to her ears.

"Tra la, tra la! I'm not listening to you, Elvira. I was so unhappy at supper when he barely looked my way, but this makes up for it. I *must* go to him!"

"I am supposed to be your chaperone," pleaded Elvira. "If you go you will compromise me as well as yourself."

"It was precisely *not* to be lectured to like this that I employed you in the first place," responded Delphine with sudden iciness and next she was off down the stairs.

Elvira continued on her way to bed.

Doubts about the Prince were beginning to trouble her mind. Surely a gentleman would not seek to so compromise the lady he loved by asking her to meet him unchaperoned in the middle of the night?

A little after the castle clock struck one she heard footsteps in the passage and stop outside her door.

"Come in," she called in answer to three soft raps.

Delphine opened the door and tiptoed to the bed.

"How do I look, cousin?"

"How do you *look*?" echoed Elvira, leaning on her elbows and peering at her cousin in the moonlight. "Why, what can you mean?"

Delphine swung round to the pier glass.

"I can't tell – it's too dark, but do I look – *different*? Like someone who has been kissed and kissed until she could barely draw breath?"

"Kissed and kissed?"

Elvira closed her eyes at this evidence of the Prince's passion for his fiancée. She knew she should remonstrate with her cousin but, remembering Serge's lips on hers, she felt she was in no position to do so.

Delphine sank on her knees by the bed.

"There's more – but I can't tell you. All I can tell you is that the Prince is unbelievably romantic and impetuous. He says he is *dying* with desire for me."

"I s-see," stammered Elvira, wishing Delphine did not feel compelled to tell her all this.

"I don't know anything any more. I can't go against my father's wishes, can I? Yet how can I refuse the blandishments of my future husband? Oh, love, love! How sharp is thy sting! But how could *you* be expected to understand it, cousin?"

"How, indeed!" sighed Elvira, rubbing her eyes.

Delpine squeezed her hand.

"Tell me what to do. What can I do?"

Elvira laid her head against her pillows. This great outpouring of emotion from her cousin made her feel dispirited.

"I suppose," she said at last, "I suppose you must follow your heart."

Delphine sprang to her feet.

"Follow my heart. Yes! You are right. That is what I shall do. Tra la la!"

She raced to the door, opened it, turned with a wave and darted out.

'*Tra la la*, indeed,' thought Elvira, pulling the quilt up over her shoulders.

She could only pray that Delphine did not plan anything untoward.

*

Next morning, Baseheart Castle was in an uproar.

Elvira woke to the sound of doors slamming, feet

running, wails of grief, shouts of anger. She sat up in bed, wondering what the hullabaloo was all about.

The next moment the door flew open and Lady Cruddock appeared, hair in disarray, peignoir unfastened, a thunderous expression on her face.

"You – out of bed this instant!" she yelled.

"W-what is the matter?" Elvira could not help but cower.

"As if you didn't know!" snorted Lady Cruddock. "As if you weren't involved!"

"But I don't – I'm not," Elvira countered, although she had no idea of the accusation.

"Out of bed and follow me *this instant*!" shrieked Lady Cruddock.

Elvira scrambled for her slippers and shawl for barely a second before Lady Cruddock seized her arm and hustled her out of the room.

"W-where are we going?" she asked tremulously.

"To the library," came the short reply.

Elvira was out of breath by the time Lady Cruddock flung open the library door and pushed her through. Her eyes alighted first on Serge by the window, his expression black with rage and then she saw Lord Baseheart, pacing the floor like a man possessed.

'What on earth happened here last night?' Elvira wondered.

Lord Baseheart caught sight of Elvira and stopped.

"You!" he snarled. "You ingrate, you vixen, what have you to do with this?"

Elvira was bewildered.

"How can I tell when – I do not know – what has

occurred?"

"My daughter, madam," Lord Baseheart's nostrils flared. "My daughter and that – that excuse for a Prince left a letter declaring they have eloped. *Eloped*!"

"E-eloped?" repeated Elvira dazed.

With a shock her passion for the Prince was finally gone like seeds blown from a dandelion. He was not the man she had imagined him to be. *Her* Prince would never have stooped to such behaviour. *Her* Prince was not a villain – a cad – a scoundrel!

She shrank back as Lord Baseheart's face loomed close, so close she could detect stale toilet water on his beard.

"Confess! You aided and abetted my daughter in this folly."

"N-no, sir. I did not."

Lord Baseheart stared with uncertainty and then another wave of despair seized him and he staggered away, hands to his head.

"My daughter is lost – *lost*."

"He will defile her," declared Lady Cruddock grimly, eyes following her brother. "Defile her, abandon her and return to France."

Serge, still standing by the window, threw Lady Cruddock a contemptuous look.

"No. He will marry her. Of that I am certain."

"Then why?" groaned Lord Baseheart. "Why does she humiliate me? Last night I announced their betrothal and so invited all our guests to the wedding. I shall be the laughing stock of the County. Why did my daughter do this to me?"

"She was encouraged, brother!" screamed Lady

Cruddock. "Encouraged by that creature there. I have the proof."

With long eager fingers she drew a letter from her sleeve and brandished it.

"Another letter, sister?"

She nodded with a certain unmistakable relish.

"I found it under that traitor Elvira's door this morning and read it. Would you like to hear what it says?"

Lord Basheart gave a strangulated assent and his sister opened the letter.

"*Dear Elvira,*

I am following my heart, as you advised.

Your cousin, Delphine.

PS. Please feel free to take my green gown and my Chinese slippers. I shan't need them."

Lord Baseheart snatched the letter from his sister's hand and read it again. Then he turned glowering eyes on Elvira.

"What more did you hope to get out of her shame, eh? Pearls – a ruby necklace – a ring or two?"

"I had no idea – what she planned to do."

"Liar!" stormed Lord Baseheart. "By Heaven, I'll beat the truth out of you!"

He raised his hand, but was arrested in his intent by the dark voice of Serge.

"Lord Baseheart! I doubt Miss Carrisford knows anything. The Prince would have been careful to keep his plan to himself. If you wish to save your daughter from the ignominy of a rushed marriage by a country parson, I suggest you allow me to set out after them. I will find them and, I vow, bring them back here to face the consequences of their actions."

Lord Baseheart regarded Serge with astonishment.

"Do you take me for an even greater fool than I have so far proved? I have never heard of a servant assuming such influence over his Master. Besides, how do I know you are not implicated in the plot? How do I know you aren't taking this opportunity to escape after them?"

Serge's expression was one of such utter disdain that Lord Baseheart drew back.

"Whether you accept my offer or not, I am going in pursuit," was all Serge said, while Elvira noticed the muscle flexing in his jaw and his hand clenched into a fist.

'He is so in love with Delphine,' she mused with a surge of envy. 'So in love that he is blinded to the impropriety of a servant pursuing his Master.'

The level of his passion shook her. If only she could so inspire a man's heart, even – and she admitted it to herself with wonder – even *Serge's* heart.

"Let him go, brother," advised Lady Cruddock. "He has more chance than yourself of finding that blackguard."

'*Blackguard*,' thought Elvira. That was how Serge had described the Prince, just before he kissed her. He must have been trying to warn her not to fall in love with his Master. No doubt it tormented him that the woman he loved, Delphine, had already been duped.

Lord Baseheart now gestured to Serge.

"Go, then. And if you kill the mountebank, you will have my heartfelt gratitude."

Serge strode out, Elvira's eyes following him all the way.

"And what about her?" Lady Cruddock pointed at Elvira. "What shall we do with her?"

"We'll lock her in her room," growled Lord Baseheart. "Until such time as we learn the truth of her involvement and what she hoped to gain from the scandal."

"Perhaps," considered Lady Cruddock, "perhaps Delphine promised to arrange an advantageous marriage for her to some French nobleman or other, something we would never do by reason of her inferior birth."

Lord Baseheart gave a roar.

"Sister – I'll wager you're right! She hoped to be bettered! By Heaven, I'll see to it that she's bettered all right. I'll marry her off, but not to a nobleman."

"No," agreed Lady Cruddock, "*not* to a nobleman."

Elvira, horrified at their discussion, found the courage to speak out.

"You have no right," she cried, "to dispose of me in any such manner."

"No right? shouted Lord Baseheart. "May I remind you that your duty is to me, now that your Aunt Willis has washed her hands of you? I am as good as your legal Guardian."

"And may I also remind you," interposed Lady Cruddock, "that after your night alone with Serge in the cottage, you have no reputation to speak of? If you defy us, the whole County shall know the tale."

"It is a false tale," exclaimed Elvira. "And the old lady at the cottage will bear me witness."

"That she won't," sneered Lady Cruddock, "unless she speaks from beyond the grave."

"She – she is dead?"

"Two nights ago," came in Lord Baseheart with cruel satisfaction. "Our coach driver brought her a hamper and found the undertaker. The coach driver who has, of course, already refuted your version of that night."

Elvira cast around wildly.

"There is Serge! He knows the truth."

Lady Cruddock and Lord Baseheart exchanged a look.

"Now there's an idea, brother."

"Indeed, sister, indeed."

Elvira gazed at them in confusion. What was Lady Cruddock's idea?

"I should not rely on Serge to confirm your story," added Lady Cruddock with an invidious smile. "It might not be in his interest."

"His interest?" echoed Elvira faintly.

Lord Baseheart regarded her coldly.

"Reputation intact, as it would be if he vindicated you, would mean you might appeal to other suitors. Reputation ruined, as it would be if he said nothing, would mean you have *no* suitors. You would not find a swineherd to marry you. Leaving the way clear – for *him*."

Elvira's heart began to pound.

"Serge? He has no desire to be my – my husband. And even if he did, why would he take someone so spurned by others?"

Lord Baseheart did not so much smile as bare his teeth.

"Oh, I think I have ways to convince him to take you off my hands, even with so tarnished a name. Now, sister, be so good as to remove Miss Carrisford from my sight."

Bewildered, Elvira made no protest as Lady Cruddock once again took her arm in a vice-like grip and conducted her to her room.

She sat on the bed in despair, listening to the rusty key turning in the lock.

She was a prisoner!

*

She remained thus the whole day, only visited by Beth who, under Lady Cruddock's vigilant eye, brought soup and bread.

Elvira had no appetite but forced herself to eat. She must be strong to resist any plots of Lord Baseheart and his sister.

She did not believe that Serge would ever agree to marry her as he was too in love with Delpine. And she had no desire to marry a man whose heart belonged to another.

Late that evening the key turned again in the lock and Lady Cruddock beckoned her forth. For the second time that day Elvira was conducted to the library.

There she found Lord Baseheart slumped in an armchair, a half empty decanter on a table at his side. Serge stood at the fireside, his boots and the hem of his cloak muddy, his expression unreadable.

Lord Baseheart lifted his head and fixed bloodshot eyes on Elvira.

"They were not found," he told her. "Vanished. And I am left harbouring a viper in my house, when my own daughter is lost to me! It's not to be borne. You – valet!"

"Your Lordship?" Serge narrowed his eyes.

"You failed to find my daughter. Well, I have another task for you. Here," Lord Baseheart jerked his head towards Elvira. "Take *that* off my hands."

Serge did not seem shocked but simply regarded

Lord Baseheart coolly.

"To what purpose?"

"Why, to marry her!" hissed Lady Cruddock. "Let her spend her life as the wife of a valet. That'll put an end to her notions."

Elvira had no doubt that Serge would refuse.

She could not believe it, when he turned and considered her from top to toe appraisingly.

"I will give you a hundred gold guineas," added Lord Baseheart, a glint of malice in his eye, "if you oblige me!"

Serge stroked his chin.

"A hundred and fifty!"

Elvira gasped, suffused with shame at now being discussed like a heifer at a market.

"I would rather die," she cried, "than be offered up in this manner!"

Serge regarded her coldly.

"Doesn't that rather depend on to *whom* you are offered up?"

Elvira reddened, realising that he alluded to her recent feelings for the Prince. He could not know that those emotions were already dead and buried.

"Take her back to her room," Lord Baseheart ordered his sister. "Her mind will change after a day or two of starvation."

Elvira, prodded by Lady Cruddock, stumbled from the room with a sob.

CHAPTER EIGHT

All that day and night and all the next day too, Elvira was left alone.

Beth tapped once at the door, whispering solace, but she was unable to release her Mistress. Neither was she able to bring food, so by late afternoon Elvira was feeling ravenous.

She was curled up under the quilt when she at last heard the key turning in the lock. She sat up, hair tumbling over her face and stared hopefully towards the door. Perhaps it was Beth with something to eat.

The door swung open and there on the threshold stood Serge.

"Come," he said simply, extending his hand towards her.

Elvira cowered.

"W-where?"

"To the Chapel," replied Serge impatiently, "where the Priest awaits."

"*The Priest*!" Elvira cried in horror.

Serge's expression was cool.

" That's right. We are to be married."

"Never! Never!" Elvira shook her head wildly.

"I am not to your taste?" questioned Serge with a wry smile. "That is unfortunate, for I warn you, you have little choice in the matter. Do not underestimate the malice of your uncle. He will not hesitate to ruin your reputation, already compromised, and I will not lift a finger to help you."

"But – *you* know the truth," stammered Elvira, in utter despair.

"The truth is not profitable to me," Serge shrugged.

"The gold, you only want the gold." Elvira began to sob, as much from hunger and exhaustion as from humiliation. "You have purchased me like a – like a pumpkin at a country fair."

Serge's upper lip twitched as if with suppressed amusement.

"A pumpkin? I would rather have thought a peach."

"Do not mock me, sir. You – you – are nothing but a market trader without scruples and without pity."

Serge regarded her coldly.

"Whatever I am, I am your future. So rise and put on your shawl."

Elvira, defeated as much by fatigue as by Serge's manner, half rose from the bed, and then slumped down again with a wail.

"I'm so very hungry!"

Serge regarded her dispassionately and pulled the servant's bell. Beth appeared so quickly that she must have been just outside the door.

She hurried towards Elvira, her face filled with compassion.

"Oh, miss, what a sorry sight you are. With your beautiful hair all untidy and your eyes swollen with weeping."

"I am – so – hungry, Beth," whispered Elvira.

"Bless you, miss, I've a tray waiting in the corridor, hoping that dragon would allow me in. It's only bread and cheese and a mug of juice, but it'll set you up nicely."

"Yes – yes – bring it Beth, please."

"And hurry," added Serge shortly.

He stood looking out of the window while Beth brought the food and Elvira ate greedily.

At last she pushed the tray away.

"I have finished," she told Beth.

"Then put on your cloak," ordered Serge from the window. "The Priest has been waiting this good half-hour."

Beth looked from Serge to Elvira and back again.

"Priest?"

"I am to be married, Beth," wept Elvira.

"To – to whom?" asked Beth in amazement.

"To – to *him*. Serge."

Beth stood speechless, mouth open, until Serge motioned her away.

"Take the tray and go, Beth. Your Mistress has no need of you for the present."

Poor Beth, who had secretly dreamed of a more elaborate wedding for her Mistress, was roused.

"She can't go to the Chapel and not look her best," she protested. "And you're no fit husband if you say she should."

"See to her, then. But be quick about it," urged Serge reluctantly.

Swiftly Beth attended to Elvira's hair, while Serge watched as she brushed the lustrous tresses. All the while Elvira sat in utter silence, as tears poured down her face.

Beth fixed the tortoiseshell clasp to Elvira's hair, straightened the collar of her dress and stood back to regard her work.

"If I could put on her coral dress," she began, but Serge cut her short.

"That is all, Beth. Please go."

Numbly Beth took up the tray and moved to the door.

"God bless you, miss," she said, as she departed, tears in her eyes.

"Now, madam!" Serge motioned Elvira to her feet.

Elvira rose, wiping her cheeks with the back of her hand as she picked up her cloak. All struggle had gone out of her. She was too weary to do anything other than obey Serge's voice of authority.

In a daze she followed him out of the room and along the corridor.

They passed no one. The castle seemed eerily quiet, though it was not yet six o'clock. Candles along the walls threw flickering shadows across their path.

Serge strode ahead followed by Elvira in his wake.

The steps down to the Chapel were only dimly lit. Serge waited and took Elvira's hand to lead her. His grip was firm and her small hand seemed lost in his.

At the bottom of the winding stone steps waited Lady Cruddock. She frowned as they appeared.

"What took you so long?" she demanded. "I suppose the fool put up a fight of sorts? Did you have to beat her?"

"No doubt you would find it satisfying if I had," replied Serge with such obvious dislike that Elvira raised her heavy eyes with wonder.

"I would find it satisfying if you had wrung her neck," retorted Lady Cruddock, "but since you haven't, let us proceed. The Priest has waited so long I will not answer for his mood."

"His mood is of no importance," remarked Serge, "so long as he does the job he is paid to do." He looked around. "Lord Baseheart does not deign to attend?"

"He is sick in heart and body. I shouldn't wonder if the humiliation of his daughter's flight didn't kill him all altogether."

Serge did not answer and Lady Cruddock turned her attention to Elvira.

"I've brought you this."

Elvira gazed at the yellowing gauze veil that hung from Lady Cruddock's fingers. No doubt it had been dug up from some old trunk in the attic and as she bent her head so it might be affixed, she even caught a whiff of must and mothballs.

'My wedding veil,' she thought bitterly. 'If Aunt Willis should witness this!'

"And here, take these" added Lady Cruddock, thrusting a wilted bunch of violets into her hand. "You shan't be able to claim we made no effort on your great day!"

Elvira took the sad bouquet and through the veil she watched as Lady Cruddock thrust open the Chapel door and marched down the aisle to sit in the front pew.

A wrinkled ancient Priest stood with his back to the altar, straining his neck upward as if his collar was too tight.

Serge grasped Elvira's hand roughly and led her in.

They had just reached the altar steps when they heard loud footsteps on the winding stairs that led down to the Chapel.

Turning, they could see Lord Baseheart appear at the head of the aisle.

He came unsteadily forward and threw himself down beside his sister, wiping his brow with a large linen handkerchief.

"How could I miss the spectacle of that upstart being put in her place," he grunted, loud enough for Elvira to hear. He gave an evil chuckle. "Married to a valet. Ha ha ha."

The Priest gave an gruff cough and the ceremony began.

It all seemed a dream to Elvira, a dream whose significance she could not fathom. It was happening to someone else, not to her. The delicate world she had constructed around her was shattered.

There was nowhere else to go but into Serge's arms, although he was no more than a stranger. A man who had bartered for possession of her body could not expect to win her heart.

As she whispered her replies to the Priest, tears brimmed and fell.

Then it was over. She and Serge Lacombe – the first time she had heard his surname – were pronounced man and wife.

"You may kiss the bride," she heard the Priest say.

Serge, who had stood austerely and unyielding throughout, his voice expressionless, now turned and lifted Elvira's veil.

His gaze was so unexpectedly tender that she caught her breath, wondering if he imagined her to be Delphine. Leaning close, he gently placed his lips on first one, then the other, of her bruised eyelids. After which, taking up a corner of her veil, he gently dried her wet cheeks.

There was an angry stir from behind him that indicated displeasure on the part of the two witnesses. It was not part of their plan that Serge should exhibit anything approaching warmth towards his bride. She was to be humiliated, beaten, neglected and not cherished!

As if recognising their venomous wishes, Serge drew away and looked impassive. Elvira wondered why he was so deferential and then remembered.

He had not yet been paid for his services and her heart hardened against him yet again.

*

There was to be no wedding breakfast.

A rickety cart with a skinny nag was provided for their departure from Baseheart.

Beth had been busy throwing clothes for Elvira into a carpet bag, which was already roped onto the cart when the couple came out onto the castle steps.

Lord Baseheart and his sister followed.

The night air was cold and the snow still lay packed and white. Elvira heard it crackle beneath her heels as she crossed to the cart in a daze.

Serge helped her up to the seat and then made his way back to the steps.

Elvira flinched as she saw Lord Baseheart press a fat leather pouch into Serge's hand. He weighed the pouch in his palm, threw it in the air and thrust it in his belt.

"And cheap at the asking," snarled Lord Baseheart.

"We have no desire to know whither you are bound," crowed Lady Cruddock. "Take her to the devil for all we care."

Serge gave a low bow.

"Your concern is admirable," he muttered, and, turning on his heels, came back down the steps. Elvira watched him from under lowered lids.

His was a strong elegant figure of that there was no doubt.

He leapt onto the cart and took up the reins. At the last minute Beth came running down the steps with a basket.

"Some provisions," she breathed, thrusting the basket into Elvira's hand.

She gave a faint smile.

"Beth – thank you. If – if I can ever send for you – I will."

"I'll go anywhere to serve you, miss," whispered Beth. "Goodbye now and may God go with you."

The cart pulled away. Elvira did not want to look back, but she suddenly craned her head round.

Lord Baseheart and his sister had disappeared. Only Beth stood waving under the looming ramparts of the castle.

Elvira waved back until the trees engulfed the cart and nothing was to be seen but the tracks of the wheels on the white road.

She turned to regard her silent husband. She could not help but remember how his features had softened when he kissed her at the altar. If only that tenderness had been truly meant for her.

His profile in the icy moonlight was sharply etched. She had to admit to herself that, although he was not wearing a velvet jacket and white gloves, he was certainly a handsome man.

Indeed, now she thought about it, he was every bit as handsome as the Prince. In fact, compared to Serge, the Prince was nothing.

How could she have missed this all along?

She pulled her cloak around her neck with a suppressed sigh. What did it matter if she had at last discovered Serge's attractions? He was in love with Delphine, not her, and he had married her for a bag of gold and no other reason.

The gatekeeper roused by the sound of the cart hurried out to open the gates. Serge drew out a coin from the pouch at his belt and flung it to him and he caught it in disbelief.

Elvira was astounded. Serge had given away a *whole gold coin.*

He had married her for that money and now he was flinging it aside as if it meant little to him.

Was he mad? Did she have no value for him at all?

As the cart rolled through the gates she suddenly realised that she had no idea of their destination, no idea of what Serge planned for their future.

"W-where are going?" she ventured timidly.

"France," he replied shortly.

France!

Elvira's mind whirled.

"Where in France?"

"The Palace of Courel."

Elvira's heart sank. Of course. That was surely where the Prince and his new wife Delphine would eventually return. Where else should Serge go but to his Master's house where he might gaze on the woman he really loved, even though she was married to another?

Whilst she, Elvira, unloved and neglected, would be left to polish shoes or plant potatoes or whatever other duties someone of her reduced status performed!

A sob rose in her throat as she realised the role in life that lay ahead for her.

Madame Lacombe, the valet's wife.

*

Towards midnight they stopped at an inn on the London road. Serge's plan was to travel beyond the Capital and take ship at Tilbury docks.

They were led through a series of low-beamed, smoky corridors and up a narrow stairway to a room under the eaves.

Serge left Elvira to unpack her carpet bag while he went down to attend to the skinny nag that had drawn them so valiantly thus far.

Elvira threw off her cloak and gazed about her.

Her eyes alighted on the large mattress on the iron bedstead and she felt suddenly weak with dread. Serge had bought her and married her, fair and square.

Whatever he felt for Delphine, he would no doubt insist on his conjugal rights.

Trembling at the thought of what lay in store, she knelt down and opened the carpet bag.

The first item she drew out was a white silk nightgown. It was not hers and she guessed at once that Beth had taken it from Delphine's closet. She held it up tremulously and in the moonlight it looked as flimsy as a cobweb.

What would Serge think to see her in it? He would surely know that it was too luxurious an article to be hers.

She undid her bodice and held the gown to her breast. It felt like gossamer against her skin.

'I will wear it,' she decided. 'It is my wedding night, after all.'

She undressed hastily, not knowing when Serge would reappear. He would certainly not delay by ordering supper for Beth's provisions had already served them well.

She washed at a little stand which held a pitcher and bowl. She towelled herself dry and then she slipped the nightgown over her head.

It fluttered down over her body, soft as moth wings.

She turned back the bed quilt and slithered down between the sheets. They were rough to the touch, but were clean and smelt of lavender.

Head on the pillow and encased in her sheath of silk, Elvira awaited the caresses of her husband.

He did not come.

Some distant steeple bell rang out one o'clock and then two. The inn was so silent that every creak of floorboard, every whine of a dog, came clearly to Elvira's ear. But she did not hear Serge's footstep in the corridor outside.

At last she realised the bitter truth. Not only did her husband not love her, he did not even desire her!

Though no longer infatuated with the Prince, Elvira could not help but compare her own sorry state to that of Delphine – so ardently desired that her fiancé could not wait even four months to possess her.

Whilst Serge could not even bring himself to bid her goodnight.

'No doubt he is downstairs clutching his gold to his bosom rather than his wife,' she thought bitterly.

The Prince Charles de Courel was a cad and a blackguard, but at least he was a man of passion!

She fell into a fitful sleep, tears of loneliness shining on her cheeks.

Some time later she half woke to the sound of a footfall, drowsily murmured a name as someone drew the quilt about her shoulders.

The name she murmured, for it was the name on her lips as she fell asleep, was *Charles* –

The figure by her bed froze, turned and departed. Elvira barely heard the door close softly on its hinge.

She did not wake again until dawn. Hearing the sound of wheels in the cobbled forecourt, she jumped out of bed and ran to the window. She would not have put it past Serge to abandon her, now that he had his gold!

But it was only a milk cart arriving in the yard below.

Hurrying to the washstand, she poured water into the bowl and splashed her face. Then she began to brush her hair, the thin left strap of her nightgown falling from her shoulder as she did so.

She heard the door open behind her and turned.

Serge stood on the threshold, arrested in his tracks at the sight of Elvira, brush in hand, hair tumbling in a rich mass over her shoulders.

The silk nightgown clung to her lithe form, rendering every contour visible beneath the delicate weave. She blushed as Serge's gaze slowly travelled her body. His eyes met hers, held, and she saw that he too had coloured.

He came forward and raised his hand. She flinched as the wild thought that he was about to strike her raced through her mind. But all he did was catch the fallen strap of her gown under his finger and draw it up. Then he turned away.

"Breakfast is served. We shall depart at eight. I have hired a new horse."

He walked to the door.

"S-Serge," began Elvira.

"Madam?"

She wanted to ask why he had not come to his wedding bed and why he had not taken her as he was entitled to. She wanted to ask if this was to be the pattern of their life together.

Was she to be a wife in name only, until such time as he found someone he might love as much as he loved Delphine, when he would then abandon her to her fate?

All these thoughts mingled in her brain, but she could not utter them.

"I – shall be down in ten minutes."

He gave a nod and was gone.

When she finally descended to the parlour she found that Serge had already eaten. She enjoyed fresh rolls and gooseberry jam alone.

A boy then brought down her carpet bag and she was ready to leave.

The cart and a new horse stood waiting, Serge leaning against the wheel. He handed her in, hoisted up the carpet bag and then leapt aboard.

"Sir!"

A serving wench, the very one who had brought breakfast to Elvira, came running from the inn. She was plump and pink with untidy golden locks.

"God bless you, sir, God bless you."

Opening her clenched fist, she revealed the origin of her gratitude.

A whole gold coin!

Elvira bit her lip. She wondered what service the wench had rendered him that she should be so lavishly rewarded.

Had Serge spent the night in the wench's bed rather than with his own wife?

She tried to thrust the suspicion from her as after all, Serge had been equally profligate with the gatekeeper at Baseheart.

She concentrated instead on the journey before her. It would take three days and nights to reach Tilbury.

Surely Serge would come to her before then?

*

Four days later, standing on the deck of the *Salty Lord* as it approached the coast of France, Elvira was still a maiden.

En route, Serge had slept in a stable, a hayloft or an outhouse. Anything but share Elvira's bed.

Yet he was not, during the day, cold or careless of her welfare. In one town he stopped to purchase gloves and warm boots for her and he insisted she eat the meals he ordered.

He had presented her with unexpected gifts after half a day in London of soap, perfume, velvet hand towels.

'Items that hardly befit the wife of a mere valet,' she thought, although delighted to receive them.

He even asked her if she would like to make a detour and visit Aunt Willis, but she declined. No doubt Lord Baseheart had informed his sister-in-law of her marriage and no doubt he had painted her in dark colours. What good would it do to try to clear her name to her aunt?

Better to consider her childhood as decidedly past as her life at Baseheart Castle.

Despite her inner turmoil, a few days of good food at wayside inns had restored her strength.

As the ship docked, she was able to look around her with great curiosity.

The bustling docks, the vendors calling in their beautiful language, the panniers of long loaves in baskets, all made her senses reel.

'This land is to be my home now,' she told herself almost dreamily.

Serge hired a carriage with driver in Calais, so at least they could now travel in greater comfort.

That first evening in France, Serge arranged rooms at a small hotel on the road to Beauvais. Holly decorated the doors and Elvira remembered it would soon be Christmas.

In the parlour, Serge wrote a letter, which he then sealed and handed to a servant to post. Elvira supposed he was sending news of his impending return to the housekeeper at Courel. Perhaps the Prince and Delphine had reached the Palace by now.

'I will have to address my cousin as *Princess*,' Elvira reminded herself mournfully.

The letter dealt with, Serge and Elvira went to

supper. She was wearing the gown that Delphine had given her and which Beth had thoughtfully packed.

Although it was December, the weather in France was mild and the doors of the dining room were open onto the garden. Outside, a group of gypsies had taken it upon themselves to serenade the guests.

Serge ordered veal and a bottle of wine. Sipping from her glass, Elvira's thoughts wandered to the evening of the ball, when Serge had discovered her dancing alone on the terrace.

Why, she had been wearing this very dress!

As if reading her thoughts, Serge rose and gently drew her to her feet.

"Let's dance," he murmured.

Pressed to his bosom, Elvira suddenly found herself much happier.

The lovely melody, the scent of the fire and the beams of the other guests as their eyes followed them about the floor, all contributed to her sense of well-being. One or two of the guests called out and Elvira raised her head questioningly to her husband.

"W-what are they saying?"

"They are saying that we make a beautiful couple."

Elvira's heart swelled, her blood began to race. *A beautiful couple.* Why, so they were.

She could see their reflection in the gilt mirror on the wall of the dining room. Her face was flushed a delicate rose colour and Serge, well – he looked so – so *noble.*

Suddenly she longed for his touch, longed for his lips on hers. She longed to be enveloped by him and to yield to his ardent embrace.

Thinking like this, she could not resist uttering a heartfelt sigh.

Serge stiffened. He stopped dancing and held her at full arm's length, his expression cold.

"Tell me, madam, is it that you would rather be with the Prince?"

Stung at his misreading of her present mood, Elvira answered with equal coldness,

"Tell me, sir, is it that you would rather be with your gold?"

Serge gave an icy laugh and relinquished his hold.

"I gave all the gold away at the first inn we stopped at, dear wife."

Elvira saw once again the serving wench opening her fist to reveal the gold coin. Had that coin merely been one of a whole hoard the wench had received?

"Was a night with a serving girl worth that much then?" she asked with undisguised bitterness.

Serge's features darkened. Reaching forward, he gripped her arm so tightly that she gave a little cry.

"How could you possibly think that of me?" he demanded through gritted teeth.

"What must I think?" she cried, "when you do not come to your wife's bed?"

They stared at each other wildly. The music had stopped and the other guests were staring, perplexed at their unexpected change of mood.

"I will come to my wife's bed," grated Serge in a low angry voice, "when she is happy to be embraced by a commoner rather than a Prince."

Elvira was too enraged to reveal the truth – that she

had long ago ceased to care for the Prince and that her heart was there for the taking.

"You were a brute and an oaf when you kissed me at Baseheart," she parried haughtily, "and you are a brute and an oaf still."

She turned on her heel and ran to her room and turned the key in the lock.

That Serge had pursued her was apparent a moment later, when his fists pounded the door.

"Let me in, Elvira. This instant! I am your husband. Let me explain."

"Never," retorted Elvira, head high. "Even if you changed your mind and begged me to be yours, Serge Lacombe, I swear I would never yield now. Never."

There was silence beyond the door and next the sound of footsteps retreating.

Elvira sank onto the bed, trembling in every limb.

She had almost begun to love Serge, but that was gone. Now she hated him, hated him with each and every fibre of her being!

CHAPTER NINE

The next morning Serge handed her into the carriage without a word. He made sure the bags were secure and climbed in beside her.

After a few moments of stony silence Serge turned to Elvira with a sigh.

"Do you now wish to discuss our disagreement last night?"

Elvira turned her head to the window.

"We have a whole lifetime to do so," she replied bitterly, staring out at the larches that lined the road.

Serge drew in his breath but said no more.

Mere cool pleasantries were all they exchanged for the rest of that day.

Elvira occupied herself in surveying the unfamiliar scene that unfolded beyond the carriage window.

The houses seemed quaint with their pitched roofs and strings of onions and garlic by the door and villages with cobbled squares and stalls selling peppered meats and huge blue veined cheeses.

A rather grand coach drew level with theirs and a gentleman gazing from the window, opened his eyes wide when he saw Elvira. He raised his hat with a flourish.

"*Une femme trés belle*!" he called.

Serge opened his eyes with a frown, leaned forward and slammed the window shut. Then he rose and thumped loudly on the roof urging the driver to hurry on.

Elvira was speechless with embarrassment and fury.

Their driver was quite astonished at the frostiness between them when they stopped for refreshment. He shook his head to himself as he watched them drink their soup in utter silence.

"*Les anglais*! Poof!"

That night passed as every night since Baseheart. Elvira sleeping alone and Serge finding his own rest somewhere else. Her suspicion that her husband's bed was never as lonely as her own continued to torment Elvira.

She hated him, she did not want him, yet – she wanted him to want *her*. It was unjust that Delphine should inspire passion in two men while she, Elvira, inspired passion in none.

She was not consoled by the idea that if he played false to her he also played false to Delphine. Aunt Willis had often told her that such was the nature of men that they took their pleasure where they found it. If Serge could not have Delphine, he would have another.

That he did not choose Elvira as that other was a source of humiliation.

At breakfast she scoured the face of her husband when the serving girl entered, trying to detect some evidence of conspiracy between the two. The girl was comely and saucy and Elvira felt sure she was trying to catch Serge's eye.

To his credit he did not look up once from the news

sheet he was reading. Elvira felt triumphant until the serving girl gently lifted his bowl, her eyes meanwhile taunting Elvira over the rim.

Elvira squirmed but held her tongue, not wishing to reveal her displeasure to Serge. He might well mistake it for jealousy.

'And I am *not* jealous,' she told herself. 'I am only conscious of the proprieties that should be observed between a husband and wife.'

Nevertheless when Serge finally looked up and thanked the serving girl, Elvira wanted to throw the sugar bowl at her head.

She flushed when she realised that Serge was regarding her with a faint smile on his lips.

"Perhaps you would care for more coffee?" he asked. "Shall I call the girl back?"

"I've had sufficient, thank you," replied Elvira haughtily. "Besides, I do not care for her manner."

"Indeed?"

"She was – too forward."

"Ah, madam, you are not yet accustomed to the ways of French girls."

"I should think I am not!" countered Elvira crossly. She was convinced that Serge was secretly mocking her. "What I *am* becoming accustomed to is my husband preferring their company to mine."

As soon as these words passed her lips Elvira regretted them. She had not meant to refer to the painful subject of her continuing maidenhood again.

Serge's expression, meanwhile, darkened and he said no more.

An icy rain was falling when they finally set out that

morning. The driver sat hunched on his box, looking forward to the end of this journey. By noon the rain had ceased and the sun was out, setting the drenched fields a-sparkle.

It was afternoon before the carriage turned in at the gates of the Courel demesne.

Despite her determination to remain aloof, Elvira could not repress a cry of appreciation when the Palace came into view.

Built of yellow stone with long elegant windows, white shutters and tendrils of vine wreathed round its doors, it had an enchanted air about it. It was not as grand as Baseheart, but neither was it as forbidding. It was more like a fairy tale castle.

Serge glanced sideways at her seeming pleased by her response. For the first time that day the atmosphere between them lightened.

He handed her down and she stood staring up at the delicate spires of the towers that graced each wing of the Palace.

"W-where are our quarters?" she asked tremulously, hoping that she was to live in the Palace itself and not in some outbuilding.

"You will soon discover."

The footman who answered the door was dressed in yellow livery and to Elvira's surprise he greeted Serge with the deference of a servant. He and Serge exchanged a few words in French before the footman turned to Elvira. She in turn gave a polite curtsy, which seemed to astonish the footman and amuse Serge.

A pretty middle-aged lady in a lace cap came hurrying up to them. Greeting Serge warmly but again deferentially, her eyes took in Elvira's coarse brown dress before coming to rest on her face. Then she threw up her hands in seeming wonder.

"*Trés belle, trés belle*", she cried.

Serge introduced her to Elvira as the housekeeper, Madame Gossec.

"She will show you to your room and I expect you to join me for supper in two hour's time."

"Is there a choice in the matter?" asked Elvira coolly.

"None," responded Serge.

Elvira gave a nod and, turning, followed on Madame Gossec's heels.

Expecting to be led through to the servant's quarters, Elvira became increasingly puzzled as Madame Gossec led her up sweeping marble staircases and along highly decorated passageways. At last she opened a pair of double doors and stepped aside.

Elvira stood dumbfounded on the threshold.

It was a sumptuous room with blue silk drapes, blue brocade on the canopied bed and a gold frieze running below the ceiling and painted panels depicting cupids and roses on the walls.

A silver-backed hairbrush and comb and a variety of crystal perfume bottles were laid out on a gilt-edged dressing table.

Surely this was not meant for the wife of a mere valet?

Madame Gossec crossed to a large rosewood armoire and flung open the doors. There hung an array of gowns in silk, satin and muslin.

Beaming, the housekeeper indicated that these were

all for Elvira.

Elvira moved wonderingly to the wardrobe and touched one of the gowns.

"F-for me?"

Madame Gossec nodded.

"*Lettre, lettre*."

Elvira remembered the letter Serge had written the day before, but it would only have reached the Palace that morning. Hardly time to create a whole wardrobe for her.

Besides – how could a mere valet have such authority? And how would a mere valet pay for it all? He had dispensed with all the gold en route.

Suddenly she understood.

This room and these clothes were for Delphine! Serge obviously intended that he and Elvira play at being Master and Mistress of Courel until such time as the real Prince and Princess returned.

She recalled the strange hold the valet had always seemed to exert over his Master. Perhaps the Prince *expected* Serge to temporarily adopt his role. He would not know, of course, that his valet now had a wife, who he would wish to participate in the grand game.

"*Ici, ici*!"

Madame Gossec was beckoning Elvira to sit down at the dressing table. In a daze, Elvira obeyed. Madame Gossec then began to unpin Elvira's hair.

"*Trés belle*," she intoned again, softly this time.

The doors opened and three maids entered with jugs of hot water. They disappeared behind an ornate screen and Elvira heard the water being tipped into what she assumed was a bath tub.

Madame Gossec seemed to wish to take it upon herself to brush Elvira's hair. She then helped Elvira undress.

The three maids came in and out with their huge jugs and when the bath was deemed to be full, Madame Gossec took Elvira's hand and led her behind the screen.

Soaking in the scented bathwater, rose petals floating on its surface, Elvira thought she must be dreaming.

It was inconceivable that Madame Gossec and the maids would behave in this way unless Serge was of higher standing in the household than Elvira had supposed. Perhaps a valet in France was a more distinguished position than it was in England.

By the time Elvira stepped out of the bath into a velvet peignoir the maids were laying out stockings, garters and jewellery.

At a clap of Madame Gossec's hands the maids came fluttering towards Elvira. Removing her peignoir, they proceeded to dress her.

Garments seemed to float down around her. She was turned this way and that until the maids and Madame Gossec were satisfied. Then she was manoeuvred to a stool where blue velvet shoes were slipped onto her feet.

At the dressing table, a maid arranged her hair, twisting it up into a coil on top of her head.

Elvira submitted mutely. She had never been waited upon in this manner and did not appreciate that the maids and Madame Gossec took genuine pleasure in dressing up this beautiful young lady who had arrived in strangely ugly clothes.

She could not believe her eyes when at last she stood

arrayed before the mirror. In a bright powder-blue gown, sapphire necklace around her neck, hair caught up in silver clasps, she looked every inch a – a Princess.

What would Delphine think if she saw her now!

A gong sounded far below to announce supper.

Elvira gave a start. Had two hours passed already? Glancing at the window, she saw that the sun had almost set. She had indeed been in a dream.

Holding the hem of her dress, Elvira descended.

Footmen stared as she approached the hall. She could not mistake the expression of admiration on their faces.

For once in her life, she was the centre of attention. She could not pretend that she did not like it. She did and guiltily wished it might last forever.

The same footman who had greeted her arrival with Serge bowed and opened the dining room door.

"*La Princesse*," he declared as she passed through.

Elvira could not believe her ears. Even the footman had agreed to be a part of this charade!

Inside the dining room a long table was laid with silver cutlery and Venetian glass. Winter roses glowed in tall vases and myriad candles flickered in the sconces of four candelabra.

Beneath a marble mantel-piece flames twisted and leaped through large cedar logs. The dancing light was reflected in the blades of two silver swords hanging on the wall near the head of the table.

A gentleman standing by the fireplace turned. Elvira looked his way and blinked.

Surely this was not Serge?

He was arrayed even more luxuriously than herself. Plum-coloured velvet breeches and jacket. Epaulettes and white gloves. Gleaming calf leather boots. Diamond rings flashed on his fingers. A decoration of some sort sparkled on his breast.

"Elvira," this creation breathed and she knew his voice.

His transfixed gaze seemed liquid and Elvira fought a sense of drowning in its depth.

"You look every inch a Princess," murmured Serge.

Elvira flinched.

"But I'm not, am I? This is just a game, isn't it? To be played only until the Prince comes home."

Serge regarded her, a strange smile hovering on his lips.

"Madam," he said softly, so softly she barely heard him. "You are mistaken. The Prince *is* home."

"He is home?"

Her eyes flew searchingly round the room and came back to rest wonderingly on the figure of Serge.

The strange smile was still on his lips and at last she understood.

The man before her, the man she had married, the man she had known only as Serge, was in fact none other than *Prince Charles de Courel*!

*

She sank onto a sofa, hands to her face.

"I see that you understand, madam."

Elvira's voice trembled as she spoke,

"If you are the Prince," she asked, "then who is – who is the other?"

She meant of course the man who had *posed* as the Prince – the man who had fooled her and everyone else.

Including Delphine.

At the thought of her cousin, all blood drained from her cheeks. Raising her head from her hands, she stared in anguish at Serge.

"For the love of Heaven," she whispered, "*who* has Delphine eloped with?"

The Prince – the real Prince – gave a deep sigh.

Elvira watched him with a mixture of loathing and awe. He looked so very distinguished, so authoritative, standing there before her. But he had tricked her and tricked her, though for what reason she could not fathom.

He was in love with Delphine! She had no dowry, she had nothing in the world to offer a Prince. And it was not as if he ardently desired her, as recent events had all too painfully proved.

"Well?" she demanded.

He moved to a red wing chair opposite the sofa and sat down.

"I had better begin at the beginning," he said dully.

"Begin wherever you like," put in Elvira tartly. "As long as it is the truth you tell me."

"Oh, you shall have the truth, madam," he promised, his voice tinged with bitterness.

He told Elvira that he was at first amused when she mistook him for a servant at the *White Doe Inn*. He had been one of those fighting the fire at the inn and realised with his torn shirt and blackened face that he did not present the picture of a nobleman.

He was on his way to Baseheart Castle to meet the girl his uncle wished him to marry – Delphine.

He planned to arrive unannounced as he wished to determine for himself whether he might fall in love with his uncle's choice of wife.

"And if you decided you could not – ?" probed Elvira weakly.

"I should have refused my uncle's wishes even though my very inheritance depended on it," he replied firmly.

He had stopped at the inn for refreshment when the fire broke out. Most of his belongings had been burned so, when he continued his journey later, he was still in his torn clothes.

He had intended to stay in Gloucester that night, but had taken the wrong road in the blizzard and so happened to come upon Elvira, struggling away from her stranded coach.

He had rescued her and taken her to the old woman's cottage. His valet, who had accompanied him throughout, was sent to fetch the doctor.

"And your valet's name?" queried Elvira, although she half guessed the answer.

"*Serge Lacombe*," replied the Prince as he drained his glass.

He had not meant to deceive Elvira, but it was refreshing to be treated as an ordinary citizen rather than the nephew of a Prince.

"The effect of such status on a woman," he told her dryly, "is not to be underestimated."

Elvira blushed and lowered her head as the memory of her night at the cottage came flooding back.

It was true that if she had known who he was, she would not have behaved in so natural a manner.

He continued his story.

His discovery that Elvira was bound for the same destination as himself and her confession of reservations about the cousin she had not met for some years, caused him to further delay revealing his true identity.

If she knew that he was Charles Rowland, the proposed fiancé of her cousin, he would learn nothing more about Delphine from her lips.

"Besides – " he added and then fell silent.

Elvira looked up and met his eyes. His gaze was so full of a sudden strange fire that she was bewildered.

"Besides?" she prompted.

"I was bewitched," finished the Prince and reached again for the decanter.

"B-bewitched by what?" ventured Elvira, her heart beginning to beat a little faster.

The Prince filled his glass. Without looking at her, he gave a shrug.

"By the blizzard – the never-ending howl of the wind – the firelight – the candlelight and the drink in my flagon – "

"Oh," sighed Elvira, a dull disappointment stilling her heart. She leaned her head against the sofa and closed her eyes.

News of his uncle's death had reached him the very morning Elvira had left the cottage. He had wheeled his horse straight round and returned to France to settle his uncle's affairs.

It was no longer an imperative to pursue his uncle's choice of bride, but he felt obliged in all honour to do so.

At the same time, Elvira had unwittingly alerted him to aspects of Delphine's character that alarmed him.

He decided that he would visit Baseheart as planned, but not as himself.

He would change places with his valet, Serge, so that he might observe Delphine at a distance. He would thus discover how she treated someone she considered an inferior – himself.

"But how could you be sure your valet would pass as a Prince?" exclaimed Elvira.

"I had time on the journey to instruct him," he smiled. "Luckily, he spoke only French, so if he made a social *faux pas*, it might not be noticed. And then – he had the costumes. The meanest actor can assume the mantle of a King. Most people do not see beyond the outer show."

Elvira bit her lip. She felt he was chiding her and it was certainly true that she had been dazzled by the image the valet had presented.

As had Delphine.

She moaned in commiseration as the real import of her cousin's flight assailed her.

The proud vain Baseheart heiress had unknowingly fallen in love with a servant!

She shook her head helplessly, barely hearing the Prince's next few words.

"It was my intention, meanwhile, to woo Miss Baseheart by default," he was saying.

"I beg your pardon – ?"

"I intended," he repeated patiently, "to woo Miss Baseheart by default."

"What do you mean, sir?"

"That I planned to shower her with attention, do her every bidding in such a way that would surely have won her, had she not proved so overawed by the mere trappings of Princehood that my valet affected. I did not for one moment believe she would be so blinded that she would fail to detect the nature of the man beneath."

Elvira remembered the man she had thought of as Serge – the man who was before her now as the Prince and her husband – kneeling in the snow to find stones at Delphine's bidding.

"You did not come to know my cousin well enough," she remarked sadly.

The Prince set his glass down and leaned forward.

"On the contrary, I *did* come to know her. As time passed and I observed her frivolous, cruel, vain nature at close hand, my dislike for her intensified."

Elvira's head snapped up.

"Your – *dislike*?"

The Prince stared gloomily into the fire.

"At first sight of her, my heart quailed. I saw what she was, in her face, her stance. I had determined to carry out my uncle's wishes, though he was dead and buried. But I could not imagine taking her in my arms, let alone taking her to my heart."

Elvira could not believe her ears. She had been so convinced that Serge – the real Prince – was head over heels in love with her cousin.

"What I had not bargained for was that my foolish valet should fall in love with Miss Baseheart and that he should precipitate the announcement of their betrothal at the ball."

The ball! Elvira relived that night in her mind.

The music wafting out from the ballroom. The moon casting a ghostly light. Serge's finger – *the Prince's finger* – detecting her unhooked dress. The way her heart had begun to pound –

Then she remembered his fist clenched at his side as Lord Baseheart informed the assembled guests of his daughter's engagement.

"You were angry – that your valet – actually proposed to my cousin?"

The Prince grasped the stem of his glass so tightly that it snapped. With a growl he tossed it into the hearth, where it shattered into a hundred pieces.

Elvira now cowered before this evidence of his simmering rage.

"I was ready to kill him!" he fumed. "I forced him to meet me later that night in the garden, where I demanded that he reveal his true identity to Delphine. If she truly loved him for himself alone, then it would surely make no difference. She could still marry him, despite her father's opposition – which opposition I could well anticipate!"

Elvira shivered, reminded of the scene she had witnessed, unbeknown to the two protagonists.

"And – did he agree?" she asked. It would be some comfort to learn that Delphine had not eloped in total ignorance of her fiancé's rank.

"He prevaricated," he replied through gritted teeth. "He loved Miss Baseheart, but he was not blind to her character. He was afraid he would lose her if he admitted the truth.

"By the next night I realised he had not confessed, so at supper I prompted him to request a meeting with Lord Baseheart. I would have attended with him and we would have revealed the whole matter to our host."

The Prince frowned before continuing.

"Had Lord Baseheart not been otherwise engaged, the story might have ended differently. As it was, the delay gave Serge time to think of a way out of the impasse."

Elvira groaned. The way out had been to gamble all on elopement and once Delphine discovered who Serge was, it would be too late! She was bound to him forever, if only to avoid ruining her reputation.

Elvira had no doubt that Serge would insist on *his* conjugal rights!

How like a lamb to the slaughter her silly cousin had gone, full of the illusion of romance, believing her fiancé's ardour too intense to wait.

Elvira rose wildly to her feet.

"Why did you allow the subterfuge to continue to the point where your valet and my cousin fell in love?" she cried accusingly. "Why did you not put an end to the charade sooner?"

The Prince leaned his forehead on his hand.

"At the beginning, I did not intend it to carry on for more than a few days," he said in a low voice. "But I – I found myself falling in love with someone other than my intended. Someone whom I began to wish might love me in return, for myself alone, and not for my rank and title."

The Prince paused and raised weary eyes to gaze on Elvira.

"How bitter it was to discover that this other girl was to become as dazzled by the image of Princehood as Delphine Baseheart. How bitter to see her falling in love with a man who was so beneath her.

"Only when she had no other option did she deign to accept the hand of a man she believed to be a mere servant. And accept him then she did, although her heart lay elsewhere."

Elvira let out a sob of anger, as much with herself as with him.

"Sir, I ceased to be enamoured of – the man I believed to be the Prince, when I discovered *his* true nature. As to the man who now stands before me – how dare he accuse me of a base passion, when he so played with my emotions as to let me believe he had married me for a bag of gold – when he allowed me to believe he did not so much as desire my little finger, but humiliated me time after time by amusing himself with every servant girl he encountered!"

The Prince rose to face her, his eyes flashing.

"By Heaven, you do me wrong, madam!"

"I *do not*, sir, I am married to a mountebank, a deceiver!"

The Prince's expression grew cold as a glacier.

"As to that, madam, let me reassure you. Since the name I gave to the Priest, Serge Lacombe, is not my real name, you are not in fact married to me at all. You are free to leave whenever you like."

Elvira gasped in fury.

"Not married? Why then I *shall* leave, sir. I shall leave tonight. And I pray that we shall never, never meet again!"

She spun on her heels and ran from the room, in her flight almost knocking over the footman who stood on duty outside.

CHAPTER TEN

Wracked with sobs, Elvira tore at her dress, trying to rip it off. She could not reach the hooks and at last relinquished the attempt.

The dress hanging loose and her shoulder exposed, Elvira dragged her carpet bag from the armoire and began to throw in her clothes that Beth had packed for her.

She would not take anything that Prince Charles de Courel had provided for his wife.

Wife! *Ha*! A fresh wave of anger shook her frame.

She had left England, come to a foreign country, all in the belief that she was at least securely *married*!

What had the Prince intended should happen when they reached his Palace – that she should be kept like a bird in a gilded cage, until such time as he chose to ravish her against her will? Like a – like a *concubine*?

She would leave this tyrant and his Kingdom immediately.

She tried not to think of where she would go once the Palace gates were closed behind her. She knew no one, she did not speak the language and had no idea of where exactly she was in France. All she could think of was that she must flee.

She wondered where Delphine and the valet were at

this moment. In some wretched hostelry in England, living on bread and ale? Or would Serge bring his hapless bride to France, where he might at least find some employment?

He would certainly not dare to come to Courel. The Prince would never admit him now.

Tying the handles of the carpet bag together, she threw it on a chair and looked round for her cloak.

The door opened and Madame Gossec entered.

She took in the scene at a glance.

"*Vous* – go, *madame*?" she asked calmly.

"Yes – *oui* – I go."

Elvira and Madame Gossec regarded each other.

"But – ze storm," cautioned Madame Gossec softly.

"Storm?"

Elvira turned her gaze to the windows. Now she heard it, a banging of shutters, a rattle of hail on glass. From the chimney came a low insistent moan.

Madame Gossec glided forward and took the carpet bag from the chair.

"*Madame* go – *demain*. *Oui*?"

"*D-demain*?" echoed Elvira. "Tomorrow?"

It would indeed be foolhardy to leave in such a storm and she knew it. Defeated, she sank down onto the bed.

Madame Gossec patted her bare shoulder.

"*Voulez-vous quelques chose á manger, madame*?"

Elvira dimly recognised the question to be about food. She gave a nod.

Madame Gossec obviously knew she had not eaten. No doubt news of the quarrel between the Prince and his supposed wife had travelled round the Palace like wildfire.

Madame Gossec departed and Elvira curled up on the bed, drawing the quilt over her legs. She lay miserably staring at the fire, tears glistening on her cheeks, tendrils of hair trailing over her forehead. Her eyelids fluttered, closed, opened again, then closed.

When Madame Gossec re-entered with a tray of milk and *brioches*, she found Elvira in an exhausted sleep. Drawing the quilt gently over her shoulders, she tiptoed out.

The night wore on as the wind raged outside, ripping large boughs from trees, sending loose objects skittering, upending the wooden drinking trough in the stable yard.

Still Elvira slept on.

The wind died down as midnight struck, though rain still fell in torrents, swelling the streams and gushing from the gutters.

Elvira woke with a sudden start as the doors of her room were thrown violently open, hitting the wall on each side with a great clamour.

She sat up, rubbing her eyes, half dazzled by the light that suddenly streamed from a candelabrum held aloft.

"W-who is it?" she asked fearfully.

"It is I," came the reply and the Prince stepped forward. His features were set, firm and determined. She shrank back in terror.

Had he come to assert his manhood – take her as she imagined he might, as the pure spoil of his venture in England?

"Get up," he commanded.

This was not what Elvira had expected.

"G-get up?"

"Yes. And take this. It is a chilly night."

He tossed a purple velvet cape onto the bed.

Elvira stared at it as if mesmerised. What did he mean by all this? Why should she rise and put on this garment, when it was long past midnight?

With an exclamation of impatience, he reached for her with his free hand and half dragged her from the bed.

"Sir – sir – you are hurting me!" she cried.

He released his grip and stood back, candelabrum held high.

"My apologies," he said, but curtly. In the fluttering candlelight his eyes took in her dishevelled state, the half torn dress hanging low and exposing her bare shoulder.

His gaze was so unmistakably full of desire that Elvira was alarmed. Quickly she wrapped the velvet cape about her to hide her semi-nakedness.

"W-what do you intend?" she enquired tremulously.

The Prince gave a cold laugh.

"This, madam. Since I have been paid to take you, take you I will."

"T-take me?"

"As wife," he snapped. "Now come at once. Madame Gossec and the Priest await."

"And if I refuse?" screamed Elvira.

The Prince grasped her face with his free hand.

"Don't be a fool," he hissed. "You have been seen with me in so many places, passed so many nights on the road as my wife. You must marry me or be ruined. And ruin you I would *not*."

Her mind in a whirl, all resistance fled and Elvira

followed him from the room.

Since he had declared that he would not ruin her, he must have always intended to marry her, waiting until the moment when he might reveal his identity, as well as the moment when she had the least opportunity to refuse – such as now, far from home and in his power.

For the first time she saw his refusal to share her bed at various inns for what it was – an honourable desire not to take advantage of her when they were not in fact married as she had believed.

She realised that Madame Gossec had been sent by the Prince to ensure that she did not leave. In the interim, while she slept, he had hastily summoned a Priest.

He was determined to marry her and hopefully thus prevent her departure.

Her head began to swim as she realised that *he wanted her and had always wanted her*!

Once again a midnight wedding and once again she had neither bridesmaids nor matron of honour. There was no Beth to minister to her, but she must be married with hair awry and eyes heavy with sleep – as before she had no wedding gown, but only a torn gown and velvet cape.

Yet Elvira's tread was lighter on this occasion, her heart less heavy.

Madame Gossec, eyes brimming, handed Elvira a fresh bouquet, obviously picked by lantern while the storm raged. She took it gratefully and lowered her head to drink in its sweet, rain-drenched scent.

Father Leduc, roused from his bed at midnight, his cassock damp and his hair dripping after his gallop through the storm, seemed nevertheless in good humour as they advanced along the aisle. He beamed as they knelt before him.

Elvira softly repeated Father Leduc's words, the same words she had uttered only a few days before but in another country, another life.

The Prince produced two rings, one for himself and one for Elvira. Each was of pure gold, inscribed with the Courel crest.

It seemed but an instant before she and the Prince were pronounced man and wife.

This time, when the husband kissed his bride, his lips fiercely met hers.

So long did he kiss her and so deeply that she felt she would faint.

She heard a groan deep in his throat and knew that this was his desire for a long time. His coldness had been assumed, an air of authority he deemed necessary to make her obey him.

"Now I have you forever," he whispered in her ear.

Madame Gossec clapped as at last they drew apart.

The Priest gave his blessing and made to depart, anxious to return to his warm bed, but Madame Gossec insisted he take some refreshment in the kitchen. When she added that there was a fine venison stew and a bottle of brandy waiting, Father Leduc was convinced.

Seizing her hand the Prince led Elvira upstairs to the dining room.

She gasped when the doors were thrown open.

A wedding breakfast had been organised. Flowers in profusion adorned the table, which was covered in an ivory lace cloth from end to end. Champagne stood in glittering silver ice-buckets.

As Elvira advanced, a group of musicians struck up

the wedding march.

The Prince indicated her place at the table. On her plate sat a parcel, wrapped in Chinese silk and tied with an white ribbon.

She opened it with trembling fingers. Inside lay a ruby and diamond necklace of such rare beauty that she reeled.

"It belonged to my mother," the Prince told her.

"She was English, I believe?"

"Yes."

"So when you – as Serge – told Lord Baseheart that the Prince had been brought up in England, you meant yourself?"

"I did. My French father, the late Prince de Courel's brother, died young. My mother remained in France, but sent me to school in England and I only returned to France for the holidays."

Elvira lifted the necklace from its box.

"May I?" said the Prince softly, taking it from her.

Knowing what he intended, Elvira let the cape slither from her shoulders and the Prince delicately laid the necklace around her swan-like neck and fastened the clasp.

"Beautiful," he breathed as he stepped away to admire his handiwork. He moved to a chair at the other end of the table and raised his glass.

"To my bride!"

Elvira raised her own glass, surveying the Prince over the rim. He was her husband now and she was his *real* wife.

A few hours earlier she had hated him. Now she

could barely repress a thrill of anticipated pleasure at the thought that he would, at last, make her his wife in more than name only.

At the idea of lying in his arms, yielding herself utterly to his desire, a blush suffused her cheeks.

The doors flew open and two bewigged footmen appeared, carrying a large plate on which lay a suckling pig. Other servants appeared with plates of asparagus, steaming artichoke, *foie gras*, as well as bowls of candied fruit and glasses of sherbet.

Elvira was hungry and fell to with relish and the Prince smiled at her from the other end of the table.

"I am so glad you are enjoying your wedding breakfast, my darling."

Elvira gestured at the groaning table.

"There is so much. It is every bit as lavish as – " Her words died away and the Prince finished for her,

" – as a supper at Lord Baseheart's?"

Elvira nodded,

"My uncle certainly thought he was not wealthy enough and was convinced I must marry money," mused the Prince. "But in fact, the Courel estate is rich enough to support a very grand life, if one manages it well. You shall not go without, dearest creature. Your wish is my command."

Elvira's head swam with sudden happiness.

"Then may I – "

"Yes?"

"May I send for Beth? And may I invite – Aunt Willis to stay?"

The Prince let out a laugh of delight.

"Granted! You might have asked for anything – gowns of silk, emeralds, tiaras – but you ask for Aunt Willis and Beth! This is why I love you so much, Elvira.

"When Lord Baseheart offered to sell you for a hundred guineas, I accepted because I felt I could not leave such a precious darling as you in their clutches any longer. I did not reveal my identity until we had arrived here, because I hoped you would begin to care for me for myself alone.

"I hope that tonight you will at last accept my love. I hope that no other man's name – will be in your mind – as I make you mine."

Elvira dropped her fork in dismay.

Despite her denial hours earlier, he still believed she loved the impostor Prince. Now she had discovered he was the Prince, how could she ever convince him that she at last loved him?

She rose, determined to cry out that the man she thought she had loved, the man who was in fact the real Serge had never been farther from her thoughts than now.

Before she could open her lips, however, a great peel rang out through the Palace.

The Prince froze, his face grown pale, as if he sensed imminent disaster.

"It appears we have guests," he muttered in low troubled tones.

The peel rang out again. There was the sound of hurrying footsteps, doors thrown wide, voices.

The Prince rose and leaned his hands on the table, waiting.

The doors to the supper room flew apart. Turning to see who was there, Elvira sank down in horror.

There on the threshold stood two wretched figures, a man and a woman.

Their clothes were bedraggled, their hair sopping wet and their faces bloodless with fatigue.

The woman's dress trailed behind her, torn and spattered with mud. Leaning on her companion's elbow, she turned her dull eyes on Elvira and gave a start.

"C-c-cousin!" she stammered.

Elvira's hand flew to her mouth.

There before her stood Delphine, so cast down in form and feature that she would not even have been recognised by her own father!

*

The Prince's eyes were trained like a hawk on Delphine's companion, who was of course no other than the hapless Serge.

"This I have been expecting," the Prince murmured, almost to himself. "I had hoped, though, that it would not be tonight."

His tone was so imbued with despair that Elvira turned wondering eyes on him.

"Sir?"

The Prince did not seem to hear. His head dropped for a moment onto his breast. Elvira saw his fist clench at his side, just as it had that night of the ball.

"What chance did I have but tonight?" he mumbled.

In an instant she understood.

He had hoped that tonight with his embrace and taking her body to his, he would drive out the last vestige of feeling for the man she had once thought was the Prince.

He was afraid that the sight of the valet Serge, the impostor Prince, would rekindle Elvira's old love.

Her eyes flew to the figure of Serge. He looked so abject, so ragged, how could the Prince possibly imagine she might desire him?

Perhaps he feared she might take pity on him and pity was so perilously close to love her husband feared he might lose her before he had possessed her.

"Monsieur," whimpered Serge plaintively.

The Prince recovered his poise. He straightened and beckoned him forward.

Serge, loosening Delphine's hold on him, stepped forward unsteadily and spoke in low urgent tones. His hand gripped his stomach in such a way that Elvira realised he was begging for food.

The Prince listened with a stony expression.

"What shall I do, Elvira?" the Prince asked suddenly. "Shall I invite our guests to sit down – with us, or shall I turn them away?"

Delphine, hearing these words, sank with a piteous cry to the floor. Immediately, Elvira rushed forward.

"They must stay," she called over her shoulder, as she helped her cousin back onto her feet.

"You hear that, Serge?" The Prince's voice was dark and Elvira turned in dismay. "My wife wishes you to be our guests."

Delphine, clinging to Elvira, looked up into her face.

"W-wife?"

The Prince gave a bitter laugh as he resumed his seat.

"Yes, wife."

Serge was looking hopefully from the Prince to Delphine. Now he brightened as the Prince offered him a place at the table and he beckoned to Delphine, who limped forward, her hand on Elvira's shoulder.

"You are truly married, my cousin Elvira?" she whispered.

"I am married," confirmed Elvira, in a firm voice that she hoped would placate the Prince.

It did not.

Moodily her husband drew a glass towards him and filled it for Serge.

"There," he said. "And for Delphine, another glass. You may drink a toast to us at our wedding breakfast."

Serge, wolfing down a piece of suckling pig, did not fully understand. He grinned anyway and wiped his mouth on his sleeve.

Delphine, sinking down beside him, picked up a napkin and gave it to him without a word.

Elvira regarded her cousin with compassion.

"W-what has been happening to you?"

"Everything," she replied bitterly. "Everything and nothing."

"Let her eat," ordered the Prince, his features finally softening as his eyes rested on Delphine.

Elvira piled a plate high with food for her cousin, who picked at the offering and then pushed her plate away.

"I am not so hungry after all," she moaned and burst into tears.

Serge stared, fork arrested mid-air. He did not move to comfort Delphine and so it was Elvira who took her cousin to her bosom.

"There, there," she soothed, stroking Delphine's hair. "Let me send for Madame Gossec. She will bring you upstairs where you can have a hot bath and put on some clean clothes. There are plenty of gowns which were, I think, meant for you."

The minute she had said this Elvira regretted it. Delphine threw back her head and gave a terrible, raw laugh.

"Meant for me, *yes*. The old Prince wrote that he was putting together a wardrobe for his nephew's bride. Little did he know that it was not I who would marry Charles de Courel, but Elvira Carrisford!"

Elvira bent her head.

"But – you made your choice, cousin."

"Choice!" screamed Delphine. "How can you call it choice when I did not know the truth?"

Now at last Serge responded to her distress. He put down his fork and stroked her arm and to Elvira's surprise, Delphine turned and threw herself against his breast.

The Prince, who had been listening coldly, now leaned forward.

"I think Serge should tell us just what has been happening to them both."

Elvira shook her head.

"I could not understand him, sir. Let Delphine tell us."

"As you wish."

Delphine lifted her head with a sniff. She took a draught of wine from the glass the Prince had poured for her and began,

"I fell in love with – *him*," and she threw a glance at Serge, "almost as soon as I met him. Of course, I thought he was Prince Charles de Courel and he certainly knew how to woo a woman. I just wished he would propose and then, when he did, it seemed all in a rush. It didn't matter, I was happy as a rabbit in a cabbage patch. I was! That night of the ball was the last truly happy night of my life."

Delphine paused to wipe her eyes with her napkin.

"I didn't see him at all the next day," she resumed, "because he went shooting, but that night at supper he seemed not himself and then he sent a note asking me to meet him. Elvira tried to stop me. If only – if only she had succeeded. He persuaded me to elope with him, saying – he couldn't wait – to possess me.

"He was so ardent, so romantic! I was madly in love by then, I couldn't resist. He assured me that once we were married, my father would accept it. We could still have a public wedding later, if we wished. So I went along with it.

"We left before dawn. I took some jewellery, that was all. I was convinced my father would forgive me and send me money once I let him know where I was. That was before I found out that the Prince was not a Prince, only a valet. *A valet*! How could I tell my father that?

"We travelled from inn to inn, from village to village and finally returned to France. I sold all my jewellery. We had nothing, *nothing*. He could not find work and said we must return to – to this place, the Palace. He said you would give him work – "

Delphine's voice failed her. She lowered her head and began to weep again.

The Prince observed her silently.

"There is something you have failed to tell us," he said at last. "Where and when were you married?"

Delphine half raised her head.

"Married?" she repeated in a whisper. " We – are not married, sir, though I am – no longer a maiden."

The change that came over the Prince was terrible to witness.

With a roar of "*villain*" he leapt to his feet, sweeping the bowls and plates from the table in his anger.

Serge stared in fear, swallowing a mouthful of meat in one gulp.

"You have treated this lady dishonourably!" the Prince screamed, pointing at Serge. "On your feet, man."

The Prince reached for the two silver swords on the wall behind him. Throwing one to Serge, who caught it in trembling hands, he challenged him to a duel.

Both Elvira and Delphine cried out in horror as the men set to.

The Prince was the fitter and his rage drove him on. Serge was, however, in fear for his life.

The battle went now in the Prince's favour, now in Serge's.

Elvira cried out as Serge with a devious thrust drove the tip of his blade into the Prince's right arm. He barely flinched, but flew all the more mercilessly at his opponent.

At last he disarmed him and Serge fell, the Prince's sword at his neck.

The Prince's eyes so blazed that it seemed as if he would not hesitate to drive the blade in.

"No, no!" howled Delphine. Rushing forward, she threw herself across Serge's body. "I love him. Do not kill him, *please*."

The Prince straightened and flung his weapon across

the room.

"He is pardoned. But on one condition and one condition only. That he marry you forthwith."

The commotion had brought footmen and maids to the door, Madame Gossec amongst them. Now she thrust her way through the crowd, taking all in with a glance.

The Prince spoke to her in French. Hearing the name 'Father Leduc' Elvira surmised that he was asking if the Priest was still on the premises.

Madame Gossec nodded and the Prince motioned to Serge and Delphine.

"This lady will now take you to a Priest," he told Delphine. "Then Madame Gossec will prepare a room for you. For your sake only, Miss Baseheart, I will find employment for Serge at the Palace. He was always a conscientious employee and I blame myself for putting him in the way of such temptation in the first place."

He could say no more.

Swooning from loss of blood, he sank to his knees.

Madame Gossec made to move to his side, but it was Elvira who reached him first.

Snatching up a napkin, she quickly bound his arm and cradled his head against her breast.

"Don't die," she moaned. "*Don't die*, sir. I love you. I realise now I have loved you from the first – as servant and as Prince."

She would have said more, but the Prince raised her hand and pressed it to her lips.

"No more, no more," he murmured weakly. "Till we are alone."

Rising with her aid, he told the onlookers that he was recovered. Madame Gossec, reassured, beckoned to

Delphine and Serge to follow her.

Delphine in her turn helped Serge to his feet and the two stumbled to the door in Madame Gossec's wake. At the threshold Delphine turned to survey Elvira.

"So I end up with the servant, cousin," she said bitterly, "while you have married a Prince."

"Not a Prince," Elvira admonished her softly. "I have married a man, a man who I love with all my heart."

The doors closed on the onlookers, Madame Gossec and the two hapless lovers, while the Prince turned dark and loving eyes on Elvira,

"Come," he beckoned, holding out his arms, "I will carry you to our wedding bed."

Elvira looked anxious.

"You cannot, sir. Your arm!"

The Prince swore softly under his breath.

"My wound will not prevent me! Your love gives me strength!"

Sweeping Elvira up and against his chest, he moved to the door.

"B-but sir," she continued to protest. "You have lost a lot of blood and must not exert yourself."

The Prince, kicking open the door, pressed his face into her hair and breathed deeply.

"Nothing will prevent me from claiming my prize," he moaned. "Nothing."

Slowly, he mounted the staircase, Elvira's hands around his neck. All the way he whispered such endearments of love and devotion that her body began to writhe in anticipation.

The Prince paused before two large doors, embossed

in gold with the Courel crest.

"What room is this?" asked Elvira, her lips against his cheek.

Carefully the Prince reached down and opened one of the doors. The other he manoeuvred open with his shoulder and Elvira's eyes settled on an expansive canopied bed.

"The Bridal Suite," announced the Prince. With his body he closed the doors and carried her to the bed.

Laying her down he began to unbutton his linen shirt.

"It has taken us so long to reach this wonderful moment," he sighed, his voice choking with desire. "But now I can see it was *the perfect way to Heaven*."

One knee on the bed beside her, he leaned down.

Her arms rose to receive him, her heart opening like a flower to the demands of love.

The strength of his desire took her breath away.

"S-sir – I love and adore you – ," she murmured and then at last she was his for Eternity and she would never leave Heaven.